The Deal-Breaker

Holly Whitworth

ISBN 9798836440435

Chapter one

Emma

"Next," yells out the barista, and I step up to the counter to tell her my order.

"Good morning. I'll take two iced Vanilla Lattes. Large, Please," The Brew House is one of my favorite places to grab a coffee. It is a small family-owned shop here in New York. I like to stop here most mornings; I'm not running behind for work to grab a coffee for me and my friend Claire. This place has so much character. It's in one of the older buildings in downtown New York City, with exposed brick on one of the walls and the rest of the place painted black. There is barely any lighting besides a few light fixtures with Edison bulbs and the large front glass windows.

Once I finish paying the barista, I step to the side to wait for our drinks to get made. My mind starts wondering off to the list of stuff I need to get done today at work while I watch one of the baristas behind the counter make the drinks I just ordered. After a couple of minutes, I can feel someone looking at me, but when I look around, I don't see anyone who looks familiar.

"Order for Emma," the barista says, and I turn my attention back to her from scanning the room.

"Thank you" I walk up to the pickup window to grab the

two coffees, then head out the front door, hearing the bell above the door ring on my way out.

My friend Claire and I own a flower shop just down the street. It's a small, quaint place that we opened just five years ago, and at the time, it was the perfect place for us; now that we have become an established business, we are starting to outgrow the space.

Once I reach the shop, I look up at our sign that reads Blooms. Claire and I came up with the name of our shop when we were just little girls. We spent most of our childhood summers outside together growing up, always picking flowers for our mothers and neighbors and making bouquets with them. One summer, we promised each other that we would open our shop when we were old enough, and that never changed. So, here we are today, living our childhood promise to each other. The arrangements we made have come a long way over the years, and now we own one of the top flower shops here in New York City. We had features in a few magazines, and one time we had a small part on the Today show. I don't think I could be prouder of us. Never in a million years would I have imagined two little girls having a flower shop dream turn in to a reality.

Before I look away from our sign to head into the shop, I notice we got a new billboard above us that reads, Hayes Brother Reality, with a picture of two nice-looking men dressed to the nines. Baker and Ryan Hayes, brothers that own most of downtown New York City, are millionaires and are always featured on the front cover of all the business magazines. They have a reputation around here for being handsome men, who always need gorgeous models as their arm candy for all the events they attend, and they live in the most expensive apartment building downtown. I haven't ever met one of them or seen them around, probably because we are different people, not even on the same radar, but everyone around here knows who they are, and their names have come up several times with people around here.

"You've got to be kidding me," I whisper to myself as I roll my eyes and open the front door to the shop.

As I walk inside, Claire yells, "Well, look who finally decided to show up!"

"Sorry, I just stopped for some coffee. Did you see who's on the billboard out-front?" I ask Claire

"I see that. Those guys' faces seem to be everywhere these days," Claire says as she takes her coffee from me.

"They aren't exactly who I want to look at walking into work every day."

Don't get me wrong, they are some good-looking guys, but their image makes me want to gag whenever I see a picture of them. They have a reputation for being womanizers, everyone wants to be with them, and I have seen them with every supermodel in the city. They have been on the front of newspapers at least once a week with a different woman. They are untouchable when it comes to women like Claire and me. Not that I would want anything to do with them anyways.

I set my stuff down in the office at the back of the shop. I sit in our office chair and turn on our desktop computer to see what orders we have for the day while throwing my long blonde hair into a ponytail. It's the middle of summer, this isn't a hectic time of the year for us, but we still have plenty to get done today.

Claire comes into the office just as I finish up at the computer. "You want to go out for drinks tonight after work? James is busy with work tonight, and I figured it's been a while since you and I went out."

James happens to be Claire on again, an off-again boyfriend she has had for two years. He has cheated on Claire a few times, but she always finds a reason to return to him. Claire is the type of person that can forgive someone very quickly no matter what kind of wrong they do to her. Bless her heart, it has gotten her into some challenging situations, but she always seems to get through it with my help.

"You know I won't turn you down. I could use a night out, just us. What's it been six months since we have been out last?"

"Probably longer than that," she laughs, "we can also grab some dinner before drinks."

"That's a great idea, considering we probably won't get much time for lunch today with our jam-packed schedule."

Claire knows us well, I'm a light weight and we all know how drunk I can get if I don't eat anything before I start drinking. I'm not always down for a night out at the bar with Claire, but since she's been with James, we don't get out together anymore, and I know she would appreciate it if we had just a night to ourselves.

I'm finishing the last arrangement order while Claire starts closing the day's shop. We had our work cut out for the two of us today. I put a beautiful arrangement of three dozen red roses into the cooler to be delivered tomorrow when I heard Claire on the phone with her boyfriend in the office. I overhear her saying in a sad tone, "So you won't be coming home tonight." I walk towards the office to hear their conversation a little better, and just before I get to the doorway, she hangs up the phone. Once I know she is off the phone, I poke my head around the doorframe before walking into the office to join her.

She turns to me, her long red hair in a ponytail flipping over her shoulder and her face bearing a sad look. "James won't be home tonight, so we can stay out late if you want to."

"Let's see how tonight goes. I mean, we do have to come to

work tomorrow," I say.

We both grab our bags from the desk and head toward the shop's front door.

Once we are both outsides on the sidewalk, I grab the keys from the side pocket of my bag, and I lock the shop's front door up for the night. Then we both start making our way down the sidewalk to The Bar; literally, that's its name, that's not far of a walk from our shop.

"Want to just eat at The Bar?"

"I mean, they do have the best burgers, and I am starving right now," I laugh

We are on our way to the bar when I think we should've stopped by our apartments to change clothes for a second. We wore jeans, plain white V-neck shirts, white sneakers, and our hair in ponytails for work today. It's our typical work attire since we don't have any unique uniforms for work. We don't look terrible, but we also don't look like were going out for a night. Our apartment building isn't far from us, but maybe I shouldn't mention stopping there to Claire, just in case James was lying about not being home. I don't want to make her worry about him any more than she already does.

Claire and I once shared the same apartment, but when she met James, he somehow talked her into getting an apartment with him. She settled for the same apartment building because some days, she still needed her best friend nearby. I was delighted she decided to stay close to me, considering she is the only person I have here.

We are almost at the bar when Claire finally mentions that she thinks James might be seeing someone else again. I knew something was happening between them and this was probably the problem.

"What makes you say that?' I ask her.

"He has been working late every night for weeks. I also can't remember the last time we had sex. And you know how much I like sex. He has also been cold and distant lately. He comes into the apartment most nights and goes straight to bed without saying anything to me. Then he is gone the next morning before I even wake up."

"I'm so sorry, Claire. Have you thought about ending things for good with him?"

"I have been thinking about that for a while now. I don't think I can do it anymore."

"Well, I'll be here for you when you need me. You know that, right? You've always been there for me through everything, and I'll return the favor to you." I put my arm around her shoulder, squeezing her as we continue walking down the sidewalk.

Claire is all I have here. After we both graduated from college and moved here, I lost my parents in a car accident. It was the worst day of my life, and I took it so hard because I was here in New York City working on this dream with Claire while my parents were in Florida, living in their beach house on the coast, fulfilling their retirement dreams. It had been months since I had last seen them before their accident. Claire and I had just gotten our apartment and opened the doors on our business, and my parents never got to see any of it. Claire was here with me to help me piece myself back together and open the shop. She was there for me when I needed her the most, and I plan to be there for her when she needs me. Claire doesn't have anyone here either, so I'll be here for her when she finally decides to let James go for good.

We finally get to the bar, which is already full of people. I'm not too surprised since it is a Friday night. The hostess was kind enough to give us a booth in the back, and we were settling in across from each other when the waitress arrived, "We would like two burgers with fries and two beers, please," I told her. Claire and I always order it when we come to the bar.

"Sounds good... I'll be right back with those beers."

We both get comfortable in the booth, pulling our phones out from our bags and setting them down on the table when the waitress arrives with our drinks. "Here are these for you. The food shouldn't take long."

"Thank you," we both say at the same time.

Claire picks up her phone while taking a sip of her beer, and I know she is checking to see if she has missed calls or texts from James. To throw her attention off from looking, I ask her, "You see any hot guys here?"

She looks up from her phone and starts searching the room. "Looks like this bar is full of a bunch of duds," she laughs. We aren't the type of girls who come to the bar to look for men. I just wanted to take her mind off James for a moment.

"That's what I was thinking," I say as I look around the bar and then pick up my phone.

When the waitress drops off two shots, we are in the middle of checking our social media page for the shop. Claire and I give each other a confused look. We've never been out and received shots or anything from someone else. It is new to us.

"We didn't order those," Claire says.

The waitress bends down, leaning over the booth to us, "These are from two gentlemen from across the room."

Claire and I look at each other before I shrug my shoulders while she looks at me like, what the hell is going on?

"Tell whoever sent these thank you," I say.

We each pick up the shot glass, sniffing it to figure out what's in it. Tequila. Whoever sent the shots still hasn't made an appearance, so we tap our shot glasses together, creating a click sound, and then we tip them back, and not long after that, our food arrives. We both start eating like we haven't eaten all day, which we haven't. Then, I spot two men with their backs turned to us. They look like decent guys from behind. I point in the direction of the men, and Claire looks over. I shout since the bar is loud, "Maybe that's them."

Claires says, "you think we should hurry and finish before they come here?"

After taking a bite, I set my burger back down on my plate to pick up the ketchup, putting some on my plate to eat with my fries. When out of the side of my view, I see the two men at the edge of the booth. I turn to them, and my jaw drops. It's Baker and Ryan, Hayes.

Baker is tall, about six foot two, with dark brown hair and a little scruff on his face, handsome. Ryan is shorter, probably right at six feet, with broad shoulders and lighter hair than Baker. They both give off I'm sexy, and I know it vibes.

They sit beside us in our booth, Ryan by Claire and Baker by me. "You ladies enjoy your shots?" Ryan says with a ridiculous grin on his face. I want to reach over the table and slap the smirk right off his face, but that's not something I would personally do. My inner self would.

I'm still too stunned they are over here with us to say anything. Claire answers, "You two are the guys that sent over the shots"?

When I finally knock myself out of my bewildered state, I say, "Excuse me, not trying to be rude, but what are you doing over here?" Claire didn't like what I said and shot me a stern look.

Baker starts inching closer to me, putting his mouth close to my ear so I can hear him, and says, "We thought we'd come by to say Hello. You two look like you could enjoy some company," he leans in a little closer to me while he's talking, and my body gets chills. He smells so heavenly, like his body wash cost a million dollars, but I pretend I don't notice.

Trying to act cool, I say, "Don't you have some supermodels you left in the VIP room or somewhere else waiting on your return," They can't possibly be serious, thinking we need their company.

I don't care to let them know I know who they are and want nothing to do with them now. They may be way hotter than they look on the billboard outside the shop that I now must see every day, but I'm not about to get to know them. We are opposite people who live different lives.

"So, I take it you ladies know who we are," Ryan says.

"Come on...Who doesn't? I get to look at you guys every day all-around New York City," I say as my eyes look around the room so I can pretend I don't want to be around them. If I ignore them, maybe they'll leave our table.

Ignoring what I said, Baker says, "We have food coming. We thought we would join you for dinner, maybe some drinks," Great, exactly what I didn't want to hear.

I visibly roll my eyes. I guess I can try to make the best of this bizarre encounter. "So, what brings you two to a place like this on a Friday night?"

Baker points over to his brother. "Ryan here just got his heart broken, and so we came out for some food and drinks to cheer him up," I feel that that's a lie.

I look over at Ryan, who is frowning, "What can I say? I love a good cheeseburger to mend my heart back together."

Geez, these two have no game. If they use this to pick up girls, it's lousy and ridiculous. I return to eating my fries when Claire says, "Poor Ryan, I know what that feels like."

Claire, NO. Please don't fall for it. She would be the one to buy into what they are offering, and she's just a tiny bit gullible, which is why I love her so much. I can always joke with her, and she never gets angry.

I can feel Baker's eyes on me, so I look up at him with a smile, "Where's your girlfriend on a night like this?"

He laughs in my face, shaking his head at me. "I don't do girlfriends. I only have time for work and myself. I'm also not the type of guy who would be over here if I had one."

I can't help but think that is good information to know about him, considering that's not the guy I pictured him to be. I did expect him to spend most of his time on himself. So, I say, "Wow, time for yourself. That's what I expected from someone like you."

I feel Baker and I have nothing in common, and our conversion will end nowhere but just talking about him. I look over to find Claire in deep conversation with Ryan, and she's laughing at everything he has to say. I tell myself to stay quiet until we leave this place. I'm not open to opening up to a stranger who thinks highly of himself.

"What are you thinking about?" Baker elbows my arm, giving me a grin. He must have noticed I was in deep thought.

"Just thinking about how much I want to get out of here" I'm looking around the bar again, trying not to connect my eyes with him. If I connect my eyes with him, I may fall into his trap.

"Relax a little… let's have some fun and get to know each other. Why don't you tell me your name? You know who I am, but I know nothing about you." He gives me another grin, which does something to me this time. I didn't even realize that we had never introduced ourselves to them. I could at least give him our names, but not much more than that.

"Sorry, I'm Emma. This is my friend Claire. We own a business together. We have been friends since we were kids," I don't need to give him details about what type of business because I'm sure he'd be interested in nothing.

"Emma," he repeats my name, and there is something about how he says it. *Sexy.*

"Would you care if I call you Em?" he says. I blush and instantly want to put my hands on him because the way he just gave me a nickname was way sexier than the way he said my name. Who even am I right now?

I pretend I'm not turned on by him giving me a nickname, "Em is fine. No one has ever called me that" It was an honest answer, and he smiled like he was earning bonus points for calling me something no one else had.

I look over to see that Claire is still enjoying her conversation with Ryan. I'm glad she's getting time to get James off her mind. They seem to be hitting it off, but I'm sure she's mentioning having a boyfriend. Their food arrives, and when the waitress sits it down, Ryan tells her to bring a round of shots. Claire smiles at me like she is having the time of her life now. She might be having fun while I'd instead jump from this booth to get as far away from this unexpected dinner date as possible. Baker has a reputation I want no part of, and while he seems to be doing things to me right now, I will not give in to the temptation.

Unfortunately, a couple of hours passed, and we had a lovely time getting to know these two. Claire hasn't stopped laughing at Ryan's lame jokes. Maybe it's all the shots and drinks we have had all night. Baker has been lovely to look at, but I still haven't let him get to know me much.

I am feeling just a tiny bit fuzzy from drinking, okay,

maybe more than a little bit, but it's been a while since I have had this much in one night. We all finally decide to head out of there. It must be close to midnight. Claire and I need sleep since we have work in the morning. We tell the guys goodnight as we start walking towards the door, and thanks for taking the tab, their choice.

"Want us to give you a ride home?" Baker says as he holds his arm out to stop us from getting out the front door.

Claire and I look at each other before I turn to Baker, "That's okay. We aren't far from here. We can walk."

"Sorry, but I can't let you two do that after drinking... Claire, Ryan can drop you and Emma. You're coming with me," why does he have to be so pushy?

"But we live in the same building? You can take both of us home," I say.

I want to tell him, no, but he's right. We shouldn't be walking home this late.

"That doesn't matter, just come with me," he says as he grabs my wrist and holds it while telling Ryan bye. Claire comes up to me, gives me a quick hug then tells me she'll see me tomorrow at work.

Baker pulls out his phone from the back pocket of his pants, "I'll have my driver get us," He sends a quick text while we wait just a minute. He grabs my hand, lacing our fingers together. I got a feeling I hadn't felt before, maybe from how he took my hand like it was nothing. Then we walk out the front door in silence.

His driver is already waiting outside, holding the car's back door open for us to get in. I slide in. First, Baker got in behind me, then sat right beside me. The driver shuts the door behind us. He pulls his phone out again, types a message, sends it, and then places his hand back in mine. He acts as if this is normal for him, and maybe it's the drinks I've had that make this feel normal for me, or perhaps it's the fact that this feels nice. And for the first time tonight, I don't try to avoid whatever Baker is trying.

"Don't you want my address?" I ask as I look out the window while we drive off.

It takes him a few seconds to answer me, "Em, we can worry about that later."

I blush a little and start feeling hot. Again is it the drinks, or is Baker making me feel this way?

It is morning when I awaken to the sound of my alarm. I reach over to where the alarm is coming from, using my hand to search for the feeling of my phone. When I find it, I touch the button to stop the absurd choice of sound I chose for my alarm. My head instantly feels heavy, and I feel like my memory of last night is not good. I moan as I roll over because I am not ready to get up. I put my hands over my face to wake myself up, rubbing my eyes and resting them on my chest.

Morning. Why is it dark in this room? Wait, this is not my room.

I sit in the bed as fast as possible, using the sheet to cover my bare chest. *Oh no.* Last night starts to come back to me as I panic and realize this is Baker Hayes's apartment. I jump from the bed, saying, "no, no, no, no" as I get up. I left the sheet on the bed to avoid disturbing or waking a sleeping Baker. I need to grab my stuff as fast as possible, so I can get out of here before he wakes up. My clothes are all around the room as I make my way around, picking up all the pieces. I was able to find everything but my underwear. I will leave those as a little souvenir for him to remember me because I do not see myself returning here.

Rushing to the bathroom, throwing my clothes on as fast as possible, I peek through the bathroom doorframe and notice he is still sleeping. I don't remember his place that well, but I remember how I got in and the elevator as his front door. I mean, who all gets a fancy front door like that? Easy to remember.

Tiptoeing back through the bedroom, trying to be super quiet, I take one last look at Baker's sexy body, half covered with the sheet, his butt bare as he sleeps face down into his pillow. Do not get me wrong, last night was incredible, but I need to keep my head straight. It is not something I do. I do not make one-night stands or stay at another man's place I don't know well. Once I get out of his room, I run down the stairs of his two-story apartment, get to the elevator, then push the down button several times, hoping it will open before he finds me leaving. It opens, and I throw my hands up before I rush in with the door closing. I make my way out of his fancy penthouse building to the street, where I wave down a taxi.

I am so mad at myself for last night. I didn't want to give into whatever game Baker played on me last night, but apparently, I did. What has gotten into me?

Chapter Two

Emma

I don't think I could have gotten to my apartment fast enough. Once I closed my front door, I lay against it as if Baker were chasing after me. My breathing from leaving so fast finally slowed down. I can't believe last night happened. I head down my hall, into my room, and then into my bathroom. I start the shower, then look at myself in the mirror. My makeup is all over my face, my hair is in a super messy bun, and I'm pretty sure I put my shirt on inside out from trying to leave so fast.

I stripped down and got into the shower to wash off all the memories from last night. Sadly, I cannot wash away the scene of Baker naked in his apartment. I run my hands down my face, placing them behind my neck and letting the water run down my front. I want to think that last night was a dream and it wasn't real. Still not understanding why the Hayes brother ended up at our table.

I finish my shower, and my phones start ringing while drying off.

It's Claire. Once I open the call, I hit the speaker button and then continue drying off before wrapping my towel around me.

"Emma, please tell me you made it home last night."

"I'm home now," I bite my lip and close my eyes,

"You went home with him, didn't you, Emma? You need to tell me where he lives, what his place looks like, was he good in bed?"

I'm so embarrassed. Claire wouldn't be, but me.

I don't do things like this.

"Can we talk about this at work? I just got out of the shower. I'm going to get ready, and then I'll see you at the shop in half an hour, okay?"

"I'll see you there, but hurry. I need to know all the details from last night."

I get ready, throwing on some clean clothes and throwing my hair back into a ponytail. My phone starts ringing again, but this time with a random number. Careless scam callers on the weekends. I silence the call, sending it to voicemail, then head to the door.

Making it out of my apartment quickly, the shop still hasn't opened. I wave a taxi driver down because who drives a car when you work in downtown New York City? I could walk like I usually do, but Claire wants me there immediately.

The cab pulls up to the curb outside the shop, I get out, and then I'm quickly reminded of last night when I look up at the outrageous billboard above the shop. I roll my eyes, which seems to be something I've done a lot in the last twenty-four hours, and now I am going to be reminded every day of the foolish decision I made last night. At least I can say I am one of those girls who slept with Baker Hayes.

Claire opens the front door as soon as she sees me coming, I walk inside, and then she shuts the door locking it right behind us. I give her a look like what are you doing.

"Emma, the phone has been ringing off the hook this morning for orders. Did you see the newspaper today? It's a picture of you and Baker leaving the bar. Your name is on the front paper of the freaking newspaper!"

She's squealing while jumping up and down. I don't even know what to say, so I look at her, confused still.

"Emma, you are famous! Everyone wants flowers from us. I don't know how we will be able to do it. Look, here's the paper from last night" she holds up the paper, and there is a picture of Baker and Me, big on the front page of the New York Gazette. We look cute together. *Don't even think about it. Get that thought out of your head.* Under the photo, it says

New York City's hottest bachelor was spotted leaving a bar with Blooms' flower shop owner, Emma Adler.

I scratch my forehead, letting out a deep breath. I'm not mad that I'm on the front page. It will be so great for our business. I'm upset because if Baker sees this, he'll know where I work, and that can't be good for his reputation.

The phone doesn't stop ringing, and it's noon. We have been able to get as many orders filled as possible, but we are starting to run out of flowers. We had to turn a few orders down but promised them we could fulfill their orders next week. It's just Claire and me here, so we are already overworking ourselves for the day.

We find some time to sit down to eat something for lunch. We called to have sandwiches delivered from our neighbor's, The Sandwich Shop. I pull out my phone and notice a text from a random number; when I read it, My drunk self probably gave him my number last night. My sober self would never do that.

Baker: Why did you leave me so early this morning?

I blush. This guy can't be serious. I didn't think I would ever hear from him again. What does he want from someone like me?

I choose to ignore his text. I do not have time for this today. I will gladly take the business he has given us, but I don't see a future with a man like Baker. Don't get me wrong, he was phenomenal in bed, and today I have found myself thinking about last night, but it would never work out between us.

Claire and I had to shut the shop down early today. We ran out of flowers. Our delivery drivers ran all over New York City, delivering some of the best bouquets we have ever done. We are tired, and I want to get out of here so I can get home to relax from this momentous day.

We are both closing the shop when I realize I have several missed calls and texts from Baker. What on earth does this man want from me?

Baker: Can I see you again tonight?

Baker: Please answer my text!

Baker: why are you ignoring me?

Baker: That's it. I'm coming to see you.

We are still at the shop cleaning up, and he sent that 20 mins ago. I immediately start hurrying to get this place closed. I'm rushing to get out of here before he shows up here.

I didn't mention Baker messaging me during our lunch today, and I don't plan to tell her about these messages either because I know she'll tell me to see him, so I rush her to finish up without her telling her why.

"Come on. Claire, let's leave the rest for tomorrow. Can we go"?

"Geez, Emma, Chill. We have nothing else to do today."

"Sorry, I'm just so tired. Let's speed this up so I can go to bed."

She laughs at my response. “Bed? Emma, it’s 3 pm.”

I fake yawn. “Three. Seems so much later.”

I hear the front door open as I go to the back of the shop to put away some of the cleaning supplies. It immediately startles me; I know it's Baker. I hear Claire say, “Baker, oh my gosh, you’re here... Uh... Emma is at the back office if you are looking for her”

Crap. I hurry into the office, closing the door behind me. Only for it to open back up with Baker coming straight in behind me, closing the door behind him.

He grabs me by my wrist, pulls me back into him, and then pushes me up against the back of the door. He puts his head into my neck, where he starts kissing me all over aggressively.
His hands a placed on each of my hips, inching his hands closer to my breast.

“What are you doing here?” I spit out while trying to slow my breathing down. He came at me so quickly and intensely that I wanted to stop him, but I couldn’t.

“Seriously, didn’t you get my text? I told you I was coming to see you,” he says, moving his mouth up and down my neck and right to my lips.

We start kissing like we’ve needed this all day. His hands move down under my butt, where he cups both cheeks and then lifts me, putting my legs around him. He picks me up, carries me over to the desk, then places me down on my desk without his mouth leaving mine.

I need to get this situation under control. We can’t be doing this here right now.

I pull myself away from him, even though it’s hard to say, “We can’t do this.”

He locks eyes with me, “why...give me a good reason why

we can't."

"We just can't do this," I wave my hand between us, "right here, right now."

"Right, I'm sorry," he situates, clearing his throat before resting both his hands on my thighs.

"You can't just show up here and do this," I say as I try to control my breathing.

"I just needed to see you."

I blush. Baker can't be real. I still don't understand what he wants from me.

"I'm going to be leaving here soon, and I have plans with Claire," I lie. "Can we do something some other time, maybe?" I say that as if I want to see him again, but I'm still unsure what I would like with him.

He looks down like he's thinking and then back up to me, "Can I see you tomorrow?"

"I'll see what I have planned tomorrow, and then I can get back to you. Will that be alright with you?"

"Don't leave me hanging... please."

He picks me up off the desk, placing my feet back on the floor. He uses his forefinger to turn my chin up, looking at him and kissing me softly. "I'm serious, Em. I want to hear from you later. Don't leave me on read again."

"You will, Baker...I promise" I can't exactly promise, but I'll tell him what he wants to hear right now.

I open the office door back up to leave, him following behind me, and we make our way to the front. Claire looks at me with a massive smile, and I'm sure she knows what happened there. My flushed face probably gave it away. I join her at the front counter, waiting for Baker to leave.

Baker walks to the door, opens it, and turns to me, "I'm serious, Emma. I'll see you later," He winks before the door shuts behind him.

Claire's jaw drops to the floor, "Shut up! Tell me everything?"

"Well, uh, there's not much to say."

Claire acting like a giddy little girl, squealing, "Emma, come on...You know you should continue to see him. It could be huge; I mean huge for our business."

"I don't know if that's a good idea, Claire. I mean, he doesn't have the best reputation for dating someone. He will probably make me fall for him, then break my heart into a gazillion pieces when he realizes I'm just a normal girl and not the typical type of woman he dates. He is bad news, and I don't want part of it. Sorry"

"Emma, you can't give up that easy. I can think of so many reasons why you should, though."

"There are more reasons why I shouldn't... Let's not talk about it right now. I have only known Baker for literally five minutes. Let's go home and relax on this unforgettable day. Also, you never told me what happened after you left with Ryan last night?"

Claire gives me a nervous look, "Oh yeah... umm about that. He just dropped me off at the apartment building. No big deal, he knows I have a boyfriend."

I knew she would tell him she had a boyfriend, even though I secretly wished she wasn't. Hopefully, she will move on from James soon and maybe give Ryan another chance.

Chapter Three

Baker

Walking through the elevator door of my apartment, setting my keys down on my entryway table as I make my way to the kitchen. I open the fridge, take out the water, and sit on the long kitchen island in front of my laptop.

I haven't been able to get this girl out of my head this morning, and the disappointment I felt when I realized she was gone from my bed.

I am opening my laptop to find out more information about her. I searched her name in the search bar and came up empty. Thanks to the paper this morning, I could at least find out where and what she does for work. She must not have social media like most people, which is excellent. Hopefully, she isn't on any dating websites, either. Emma didn't give me many facts about herself last night. She seems to be guarding herself, but I can't blame her for not opening up *yet.*

I shut my laptop and take my phone out of my pocket. I'm checking to see if there happened to be any missed messages from Emma. It's only been thirty minutes since I left her shop. I have difficulty understanding my feelings towards her when I've only known her for not even a day.

There's only one thing that helps me take my mind off things. I throw on some clothes, slip into my tennis shoes, and prepare for a run. After putting in my air pods, I start going through the park and jogging while listening to my favorite playlist.

Last night started as an innocent night out with my brother. We went to our regular Friday night bar for food and drinks. Ryan and I have been working on closing a deal for months, a good deal that could make us billions. The problem is that the guy we have been trying to close with on the properties is a huge ass. This guy, Dave Riley, thinks we are utterly immature with how we handle our private lives. He told us he'd consider selling us this property when we got together. The point is we want those properties that he owns right now. We already have massive projects for them. Ryan suggested we figure out a plan to make Dave think we have it all together. Ryan mentioned that maybe we should settle down to prove that we aren't the guy he thinks we are. Just turning thirty-one is probably the time for me to think about settling. I just haven't found the right person.

So, this is where Emma and Claire come in. See, last night at the bar, Ryan knew we needed to try to close up this deal before this coming fall season, so while having a few drinks at the bar top. He said how about we find a couple of girls, make them fall in love with us, show Dave we are ready for the next steps in our lives and show him we aren't exactly who he thinks we are, and then when the deal closes, we can get rid of the girls, and go back to the single life.

I thought he was ridiculous when he first mentioned it, but he's right. We need to prove to Dave that we are better than what he thinks of us and get this deal done. He stumbled upon the women in the booth while going to the bar's restroom. Since there were two of them, he knew they'd be perfect for his plan. Once he got back to the bar, he pointed them out to me, one looking familiar. Before sending the shots and making our way over there, I knew I wanted to be the one to get Emma.

So, I need her to fall for me. Yes, I know that makes me sound like a terrible person. There's no way she will find out about the whole deal. I know Ryan won't say anything, and I won't. I need to figure out a way to get her to go out with me, which shouldn't be hard. I've been able to get women quickly. Emma, though, is different. She's playing hard to get when it comes to her, and she's closed off. She also has a great business and works hard, which is precise what kind of girl I need to score this deal with Dave. All it will take is a few more photographs with her for the newspaper and have her come to some events with me so Dave can meet her. If she can impress me, I know she can impress him.

Ryan shows up out of the elevator just as I get dressed, "Baker, you here."

"I'll be down in a minute," I throw on a pair of shorts and then make mine down the stairs.

I have an impressive apartment right in the middle of downtown. It's ample space, and the living room is open to the kitchen and the entryway. All the outer walls are lined with windows, filled with natural lighting through the daytime and city lights at night. The stairs are open to the main living area, and the place has rich dark wood. It's modern and very masculine.

"How did it go last night? Is she a keeper, going to put a ring on it?" he says while sitting back, arms across his chest, on my leather sofa in the living room.

"Seriously, Ryan. It went well, I guess. I haven't heard back from her today, but I did show up at her workplace to try to convince her a little more," I say, coming down the stairs.

"If you haven't heard from her, I'd say it's not going well.

You never have trouble with women not getting in touch after a night out with them. How many women have you had to block because they wouldn't leave you alone? Too many to count. I suggest you figure out a new way to get her," he gives me a serious look.

"I'm working on it," I say as I head to the liquor cabinet in the kitchen to pour myself a drink.

"Well, I thought I'd stop by to check out on the progress of our agreement. It sounds like you need to work harder or find someone else."

"You know this is your idea, and you find someone. What happened with Emma's friend last night?" I ask, pouring myself a scotch on the rocks and then joining him on the sofa.

"She's in a relationship already. Also, you're older and wiser. Trust me. Dave isn't going to care what I do. You are the owner of our business. You need to be the one to impress him. If we don't get this done soon, we'll get screwed at making millions of dollars. We can't give him too long to think about it. We will have to find someone else to buy from, but we both know these buildings Dave Riley is selling will make us the greatest money."

Claire has a boyfriend, they seemed to hit it off well last night, or so it looked. Indeed Emma hasn't been in a relationship lately. Is that why she's closed off?

Ryan is correct, but I don't need him to know that. I'm not going to let my little brother think he came up with the best plan for our business.

"Whatever you say, I'll hold up my end of the deal, and we'll have this guy right where we want him. Now, why don't you leave and move to a different building? I don't like you showing up unannounced all the time."

Ryan gets up from the sofa and starts towards the elevator, "I'll see you at the office on Monday."

It's Sunday, and I still haven't heard back from Emma. I'm starting to get aggravated, but I also want to see her. I want to know what she is doing.

I open my text thread with her

Me: Are you ignoring me again?

I hit send and hoped she'd respond quickly, and she did.

Emma: Sorry, I was busy last night

I feel like she may be lying, but oh well.

Me: Are you free today

Emma: I am

That was just the answer I wanted.

Me: Can I take you to dinner tonight?

It takes her a few minutes to respond, and I have zero patience.

Emma: Yes

I responded with the details and got her address to pick her up. I'm taking her to Buono. It's a nice Italian restaurant not far from my building. I wanted somewhere where there would be a chance of us getting photographed again. I am hardly ever photographed with the same woman twice, so this should impress Dave.

I pull up outside her apartment. For some reason, I expected her to live somewhere a little nicer. She made good money owning her business in downtown New York City. She didn't want me to come up, so she asked me to text her when I arrived, and she would come down. After letting her know I was out front waiting, I wiped the sweat off my palms onto my pants. I don't know why I'm nervous.

I don't have to wait too long for her. She comes right out just minutes after I let her know I'm here. I do a double look because she looks gorgeous. She's wearing a tight black thin, strap dress that comes right above her knees, her blonde hair is up in a high ponytail, she isn't wearing too much makeup, just enough to make her green eyes stand out, and she has on black thin strapped heels. How did I get so lucky with this situation?

I get out of the car before she makes it over. Then I go around to open the door for her. She says, "Hey." I must be speechless because I nod to her after she says it. I close her car door and walk into the driver's side door.

I start my Porsche, and off we go. There seems to be an eerie silence between us on the way. I'm unsure what we should talk about, so I reach over to rest my hand on her thigh, so it isn't awkward between us. When we pull up, I park out front and then go to her side of the car to let her out. She gets out and says, "Thank you." I grab her hand, lace our fingers together, and reach the front door.

"Reservation for Hayes, please," I tell the hostess once we make it inside.

"Just one minute, sir."

While we wait, I notice that Emma looks uncomfortable and adjusts her dress. I lean over and whisper in her ear, "You look stunning, stop."

Her cheeks turn flush. She looks at me, smiling.

The hostess calls us, and we make our way to the back of the restaurant to a secluded table. I pull Emma's Chair out for her, and then I have a seat in my chair.

This restaurant is one of the fancier places in the city. The walls a lined with rich wood, with just a few lighting fixtures on the walls. All the tables are covered with white tablecloths and have candles lit in the center.

The waitress appears, "What can I get you guys to drink?"

"We'll have a bottle of house red, please" I look at Emma to make sure that's okay with her, and she nods.

Once the waitress walks away, I break the awkward silence that we have to go on. "I hope you like Italian food. I'm sorry I didn't even think to ask when I told you this place."

"What girl doesn't love good pasta" she answers while looking at the menu.

I know many girls who won't eat pasta. Most of my past dates don't order food or eat what I order for them. I love a girl who eats, though. I don't tell Emma any of that, and I ask, "So what do you think you are going to order?"

"What's good here? I'm sure you've eaten here plenty of times."

I have been here on quite a few dates and sometimes by myself.

"Their Pasta Carbonara is the best," I say because it's what I order almost every time I'm here.

"That sounds great," she says as she sets the menu on the table.

The waitress arrives with our bottle of wine. She pours it into two glasses, and I give her our order. Once she walks away, I turn my attention towards Emma, placing my hands on the table in front of me.

"So, Emma, tell me about little about yourself."

"Well, I'm Emma Adler. I own a flower shop with my childhood best friend, Claire. I live in a small apartment in downtown New York by myself. I like pasta, and I'm on a date with New York's most eligible bachelor" She smiles while picking up her wine glass.

I laugh, "I know all these things. Tell me something I don't know" because I want to know plenty of things about her.

"How about for every question you ask me about myself, I can ask you one. I would like to know more about you, Baker Hayes," I smile. There's just something about the way she says my name.

"Deal," I say, not knowing what questions she will ask me. They could not be good.

"Okay, so ask away."

I think about a good question for a second, "What is your favorite thing to do when you are not working?"

"I like to take walks through central park. Most days off, though, I spend at my apartment, sometimes with Claire, watching old tv shows and ordering takeout. I'm not a very interesting person. My business keeps me very busy, so I don't get many days off. What's something you like to do in your free time?"

"So basically, you are an old lady" she rolls her eyes at me when I say it—making me laugh.

"I guess I am. Now answer my question," Emma says, taking another drink of wine before she leans back in her chair.

"Well, Em, it may surprise you, but I run in my free time. It helps me relax and clear my head. Like you, I work a lot except on the weekends, where I spend most of my time outdoors."

Giving me a surprised look while setting down her wine glass, "I don't take you as a runner Baker. I thought you'd surely be a man who spends all his money on extravagant vacations and partying."

“Well, you thought wrong. Partying is not my type of fun, which would be Ryan’s thing.”

She is impressed with me so far. We do not get any more questions in before our dinner arrives. I wanted to ask more questions to get to know Emma, but they can wait for later.

We talk about work while eating, and we finish off the wine I ordered.

“Would you want to come back to my place? We can finish our conversation.”

“Yes, that would be nice. I have one thing I would like to add before we go....” Emma pauses, then adds. “I want to apologize for the other night. I am not a woman who makes one-night stands, and I would like to say I am sorry for leading you on by sleeping with you. I may have had too many to drink that night, and I know I should not be blaming that, but I want you to know.”

“Em... there is no need to apologize for the other night. If anyone should be sorry, it's me. That night was incredible, but I understand that it is something we should not have done. Yet. How about we make a pact? Let that be something that will not happen again until we both are... well, ready for something like that to happen again. Mean something.”

She smiles radiantly, “I would like that very much. Thank you”

I appreciate that she wanted to apologize for something I should be apologizing for. That night was my fault. I couldn’t keep my hands off her once I got her back to my place. Maybe it was that I had her there, and I didn’t want to forget a night with her in case I never got to see her again.

“You’re Welcome. Anything for you” I give Emma a grin, then go over to pull her chair out for her.

We are headed out the door holding hands again. I again open the car door for her, then I get in and drive off, leaving a few photographers with options for tomorrow's newspaper.

“Would you like something to drink?” I ask her as she sits on the living room's leather sofa. “Water is fine.”

I grab two bottles of water from the fridge, then join her on the sofa leaving a few spots open between us. We are back at my place where we can be comfortable. We have only had an opening for conversations when we have been out in public places, and I want to get her to relax so that she can be open a little more.

“I'm going to slip these shoes off. My feet are killing me in these things. I don't wear them often,” Emma starts undoing the straps on both of her heels. Once she takes her feet out of them, she sets the shoes to the side.

“Put your feet up here,” I motion to the spot next to me on the couch. I grab a pillow beside me, putting it beside me so she can prop her feet on it. I grab both her feet to set them on the pillow and start rubbing them for her as she rests her back against the couch's armrest.

“Ah, you are a good man, Baker. I honestly can't remember the last time someone has done this for me. Maybe my mom when I was a little girl.”

“It's been that long. No ex-boyfriend did this for you?” I ask as I continue to give her feet attention.

“Sadly, no, I can't remember the last time I had one of those either,” she gives out the cutest laugh.

“That's a joke. How is someone like you still single?” I ask myself this question when I ask her. She seems like the perfect woman you bring home to your parents, the one you'd marry. *Did I think something like that?*

"I dated when I was in college getting my business degree, but Claire and I moved to New York City to start our business once I finished school. Shortly after we opened the doors of Blooms, I lost my parents in a tragic accident. After they passed away, I stayed focused on the business and spent time with Claire because she was all I had. I just haven't put a lot of thought into dating anyone."

I can't even imagine, "I'm so sorry, Emma," Sorry for what she's gone through.

"It's been over five years now, and I've become a stronger person now than I was then. All with the help of Claire too" she picks up her water from her the coffee table to get a drink, and I can't help but think maybe she is doing it to stop herself from tears. I stop rubbing her feet and move closer, putting her legs over my thighs. I grab one of her hands to hold and place my other hand on one of her legs. I want to give her some comfort from me, wanting her to know I can be there for her.

"We can talk about me if you'd like. Ask me any question you would like to know the answer to" I could regret telling Emma this.

She thinks about it for a minute, making the sweetest thinking face while putting her index finger on her chin. She looks at me, grinning, when I start thinking maybe I shouldn't have let her ask me anything. "How many women have you slept with?"

Ugh, we're going there already; I try to come up with an accurate number but hopefully, it's a number that won't scare her. I think about it for a second, not because of how many but because I don't keep track. "That number is twelve."

She drops her jaw, putting her hand over her mouth.

"Seriously, are you lying, or is that the real number?" I'm unsure if this is a good or bad number. Is she about to tell me she has slept with only two guys, my number two?

"It's a real number. Is it bad?" I'm so confused. Is it terrible?

"I'm impressed. I've seen you on the newspaper cover with more women than that. I expected you to tell me it was around thirty or so women."

I was beginning to think I was a man whore there for a minute. I'm so relieved she is impressed. I start laughing, "What kind of man did you think I was? Most of those photos are of people I've had to meet at work or something. I've never actually dated any of those women." There, maybe that'll impress her too.

"Wow, I'll stop believing everything I read in the newspaper from now on," she laughs, making me feel so good that I can help turn a sad moment into a funny one.

"So, what's your number then?" I needed to know since she wanted to know mine.

"Five, it would probably be higher if I didn't spend the last few years celibate because I just wasn't going out," she gives me a sad smile.

"So, you just went without for a few years? Exactly how does one do that."

"It's straightforward. Here's what you do... you don't do it," Emma's, laughing hysterically.

"Now you're making me look bad."

She's still laughing, "Sorry, so sorry. We can talk about something else."

"How old are you?" she looks younger than me but older

than twenty-five.

"I am twenty-seven. I also know that you are thirty-one."

"You must have done your homework before going out with me."

"I read an article about you and your brother earlier this year" she sits up a little and adjusts her sitting position. "Doesn't everyone know about you? Your face is on everything these days, and I even look at you on the huge billboard outside the flower shop. You are New York City's most eligible bachelor. Just having my picture taken with you helped my business."

"What do you mean it helped your business?"

"Claire and I could hardly keep up with the phone ringing off the hook yesterday. We ran out of flowers and had to shut down early for the day, all because I was on the paper's front page with you. We have had average sales lately, but if we can have days now and then like we did yesterday, we could open a bigger shop like we have wanted" Her face lights up when she talks about her business. You can tell from how she talks about it that it is her life.

"Wow, that's great, Em. I had no idea. I know a great Real Estate agent that could help you get that big flower shop. That's if you need someone to help you find one" I give her a grin.

"Well, thank you. Hopefully, one day I'll be able to look for one. I'm not sure we make enough just yet to afford a big space" she takes her legs off me and puts her feet on the floor. She picks up her shoes to put them back on.

"Are you leaving so soon?" not ready for the night to end just yet. I look at my watch to check the time, and it's just after nine-thirty.

"We both have work tomorrow. I should probably get going," Emma finished getting her shoes back on and got up from the couch.

"I'll drive you back home" I get up and follow her to the elevator entryway.

"I can catch a cab. There's no need for you to get out again," Emma turns to look at me with a sad look.

"You're crazy. I'm taking you home myself," I say with a grin.

Then we both make our way into the elevator. The doors open to the underground parking, and I hit the unlock button to unlock the doors on my Range Rover. When the lights flash, she gasps, throwing her hands up in the air. "You have to be kidding me. How many cars do you have?"

I laugh at her reaction, "I own three cars, two of them I drive myself and one for my driver, Carlos, to take me in" I open her door, she gets in, and I go around to get in myself.

"This one is my favorite," she says as she checks out the whole car and touches buttons on the screen. "I own one car I share with Claire, and it hardly gets driven since we walk almost everywhere or take a cab."

"Maybe I'll let you drive it sometime," I say as I back up the car, leaving the underground garage.

She gives me a giddy grin. I can tell she wasn't expecting me to say that.

"What! You'd let me do that."

I reach over to her, grab her hand, lacing our fingers together. "Of course, I would."

She squeezes my hand and looks out the side window. I can tell she has something on her mind. I rub my thumb over her knuckles while we sit silently for a few minutes.

"Baker," she asks just before we pull up to her apartment

building.

I look over, but she hasn't turned her attention to me yet, "Yes, Em."

"What does someone like you want with someone like me? When you saw me the other night at the bar, what made you want to come over to me? What is it about me that wanted you to have this date tonight? I'm just somebody, someone who doesn't have much money. I work at a flower shop and live in a tiny apartment."

I am instantly reminded of Ryan's idea from last night. I get this unsettling feeling in my chest; I start feeling warm. This whole time I have been with her tonight, I completely forgot about the deal, the deal I have with my brother, the brother who was the one who found her at the bar last night. She's more than what she considers herself and so much more. *Better.* I never anticipated myself to have some emotions for her, I've only known her for only a couple of days, but it feels like so much longer than that. I can't do this to her, and I can't drag her into this agreement. She's better than that. I can't lie to her about why I met her at the bar last night, and I'm not going to tell her the truth. She's worth more than that. I also can't tell her the real reason I picked her.

"Own, you own a flower shop" I have this unhappy feeling. We pull up outside Emma's apartment building, and I park. I was going to go in with her, but we should end the night here. I take my hand from her, place it on her face, rubbing her cheek with my thumb. "You are incredible, and maybe it was fate when I found you last night. I don't know. Don't ever compare yourself to someone else because of money. Money means nothing."

She stares at me with a sad face, and it punches me right into the gut. I feel like such an ass, and I should have never thought Ryan's idea was all right because it's not. It will only hurt both of us in the end. I'm now deciding the future of Emma and me, and I need to end this before we get serious with each other.

She doesn't answer everything I just told her. She is waiting for me to kiss her, but I can't. I don't want to add to something that may already hurt her. I'm choosing not to say anything about ending this, saying nothing may be better. I drop my hand from her face and go around to her side of the car.

She gets out of the door, and I give her one last tight embrace, laying my cheek on the top of her head. "Thanks for tonight, Baker. It was nice."

I let go of her for one last time, "thanks for coming. I'll see you, Em."

I watch her as she goes through the doors of her building. I get in my car with a sick feeling, knowing I may never see her again, but it's best. *Is it, though?*

Chapter Four

Emma

I walk into the shop with today's newspaper in hand. Claire is standing at the front counter talking on the phone when I get through the door. I hold up the newspaper to show her the front cover, then drop it on the counter. She tells the person on the phone. Thank you, and then he hangs up the phone before turning to me.

"Looks like I'm famous once again," I make an annoyed face.

I didn't even notice someone taking photos when we left the restaurant last night. I'm not even sure Baker did, either. I'm already tired of being the front cover of the paper. If it were me at our business, that'd be different, but being recognized for being with Baker is getting too bothering.

"Guess I'll just check the paper to see what you are up to now since you failed to tell me you went out with him again last night," Claire says, resting her elbows on the counter and looking over the article in the paper.

"He asked, and well, I didn't want to, but after thinking about it, I figured it wouldn't hurt to get to know him. He's not as bad as I thought. He was a gentleman last night at dinner. He took me back to his place, we hung out for a little while, and then he took me home. No, sleeping together, and he didn't even kiss me. It was almost like he was a different person than he was Saturday."

"Maybe he likes you," she says, shrugging her shoulders.

"I don't know. Let's see how this week goes. For all I know, he could be photographed with someone else tonight, and I'll just be forgotten. I'm not exactly his type anyways."

"You're better than the other girls he dates," Claire says, giving me a smirk.

"Thanks, Claire. Now, what does today look like?" I ask while walking towards the office to set my things down and throw my hair in a ponytail.

"It looks like we'll be able to finish some of those orders from Saturday's fiasco since we got a huge delivery this morning. Thanks to this morning's paper, we got a few more new orders". She says while following behind me.

"Great! How was this weekend with James?" I turn to her to see her reaction.

I'm so caught up in this whole Baker thing I almost completely forgot about Claire having problems with James.

She looks like she could cry, "I didn't see him. He said he had to work all weekend, so I packed his things and tonight is the night I'm ending things. I can't do this anymore. I mean, he did even come home to sleep."

"Claire, why didn't you tell me? I could've helped you." I wrap my arms around her in a hug.

I start feeling like a terrible friend. I should've been there for her. I don't understand why she wouldn't tell me.

"I just needed some time to myself, time to realize this is the end of us. I'm doing well, and I'm more than ready to get this relationship over with so I can move on."

“I’m proud of you, Claire, so no moving in with me?” as much as I like living by myself, sometimes it does get lonely.

“I don’t want to hurt your feelings or anything, but I just want to live by myself, but is it all right if I come to stay with you tonight after I end things with him.”

“Of course, you can” I go over to her and give her another giant squeeze.

We end our conversation, and I put on my apron to start working on these bouquets.

I just finished showering and threw on some black leggings and an oversized tee. I’m waiting for Claire to text me that she’s on her way. I stopped for pints of Rocky Road ice cream on my way home from work, the best cure for a breakup. I know Claire better than anyone, she may be spunky, but she is strong. She will get over this James guy and move along with her life.

I check my phone to see if I have missed any notifications, and I don’t. I haven’t heard from Baker; he was different last night compared to the man I met Friday night. It’s almost like he had something on his mind last night, but he didn’t want to share what. He was such a good man, attentive to me. I felt like we had a great time getting to know each other better. I don’t want all the good things to overshadow what kind of man can be, though. I know he can break my heart in a second, so I need to remind myself that maybe it was just a weekend fling for him. If I see him again, I must guard my heart next time.

Claire comes busting through the front door as I sit on my couch, “You won’t believe what happened!”

I jump from my seat. Claire scared the crap out of me by

coming in, in a rush, and breaking up my thoughts.

"What?" I say as I turn to the back of the couch and look at her at the front door.

She shuts the front door and then walks over to me on the couch.

"James said he was going to break up with me because he was seeing someone else, and the best part, he thinks she's pregnant" I don't think I am even surprised by this news. He was a man capable of doing something like this.

"Claire, you're kidding me. How are you holding up? Are you alright?"

"All right! I've never been better. He just made it easy, and " I don't need to worry about going back to him because I don't date guys with kids," she says, laughing.

I don't know if I should laugh with or hug her, so I do both. "Well, thank goodness you are stronger than me. I would bawl my eyes out if the same happened to me."

I head to the kitchen, opening the freezer to take out the two pints of ice cream I got. I open a drawer, take out two spoons, then head to the living room, where Claire is on the couch and is already searching the tv for something to watch. We spent the rest of the night laughing about ridiculous stuff we used to do when we were younger, finishing our pints of ice cream, and watching movies.

Almost Two weeks later...

"What are we doing?" Claire asked me with a serious look on her face.

We are both lying on my couch.

We've been hanging at my place for the last couple of weeks, eating all kinds of takeout and binging episodes of Golden Girls. Yes, we watch old lady shows, they are the best.

"What do you mean?" I give her a confused look.

"While this has been fun and all, we are wasting time just laying here watching tv and eating out every night. When was the last time we went out?"

My thoughts go back to the night I went home with the sexiest bachelor in New York City. It has been weeks since I last heard from Baker. I want to say I haven't been miserable since I last saw him, but that would be a lie. I was starting to think that we could've been something, we hit it off well on our date, but I was unfortunately wrong. He turned out to be who I thought he was. I still hold out hope, though. I haven't seen him in front of the newspaper with anyone else.

"Okay, maybe it has been weeks. What do you want to do?" I ask her. Even though I know she will want to do something, I'm not sure I don't want to.

"Let's put on our best dresses and go to Deuce," she says as she jumps up from the couch.

Deuce is the biggest nightclub in New York City that always attracts twenty-somethings on a Saturday night. All the hottest people go there for a fun night, maybe even a one-night stand. Claire and I have been there a few times before, and while she has hooked up with a few guys, she picked up from there. I have never been one to hook up with random men for a night, except for that one time, and we don't need to talk about that.

"I guess we could go," I say, even though I don't want to, but I know Claire wants to have some fun.

"Emma, we need a night out. Come on," she's always my hype girl, trying to get me to do what she wants.

"Okay! Let's do it then" I may sound excited, but inside I hesitate a little.

I just finished my makeup, which I put on more than I have. I tossed my hair up into a high ponytail. My signature looks from my date with Baker, who said I looked stunning. I have a couple of dresses on the bed when I call for Claire to help me pick one out.

She comes into my room, already dressed to go. She's wearing a dark green fitted dress that comes just mid-thigh, her long red hair pinned behind her ear on one side and long curls over the other shoulder. She's also wearing more makeup than I have seen in years. She is wearing black stilettos and has a small gold clutch. She looks hot. Any guy at the club is going to want her.

"You should go with the gold one," she sits down on the bed.

"It won't be too much," I say as I hold up the gold dress in front of myself, looking in the floor-length mirror I have placed beside my closet.

"No way! It'll be perfect" she gets up to leave the room.

She heads to the living room as I put on the gold dress. It fits like a glove on me and has a bit of sparkle. I match it with black strapped heels and then grab a black clutch to head out. I make my way down the hall. Claire gets up from the couch once I get to the living room.

"Emma, you look amazing!"

"Well, thank you, you don't look so bad yourself," I model pose it for her while laughing. She meets me at the front door.

"Now, let's go have the best night of our lives."

We get out of the taxi right at the club's front entrance. I look at the bright light saying *Deuce* in bright yellow neon colors. I breathe in and let out a big breath. I don't even know why I'm nervous. It should be an enjoyable night for both of us. Claire noticed that I had stopped walking, so she grabbed my arm, and we made our way to the line to get into the door.

Chapter Five

Baker

I'm relaxing on my leather sofa with a scotch when I receive a text from Ryan. He wants me to meet him tonight. He wants to talk about this deal with Dave Riley. I've been trying my best to disregard Ryan the last couple of weeks about this deal, but since he's my brother, it's been impossible. Honestly, I have felt like a giant ass. I met one of the most incredible women I have ever met, Emma. While I have been snubbing her, I haven't gotten her out of my mind. What I brought her into is wrong, the paper's photos and the agreement. I don't regret sleeping with her, nor do I want to forget the date we went on, but after getting to know her more, I thought she had so many great qualities that it was just so wrong on my part to drag her into this mess Ryan started so I had to do what I thought was best and end things. Ryan doesn't know I haven't seen her anymore and thinks this deal will still happen. I want this deal to happen, but I must devise a different plan.

I text Ryan, "Where are you? I'll come?"

It only takes him a minute to send a reply. I roll my eyes at his address and head out the door. I text Carlos, my driver for the night because I'll probably be drinking.

We pull up outside Deuce. Of course, Ryan would be at a place like this on a Saturday night. I make my way inside and don't have to wait in line like most people because they already know who I am. I get an instant headache from the loud music, walking towards the back of the club to the VIP section, where Ryan hangs out almost every time we come here. I spot him surrounded by blondes and a few of his friends. I head up to the round booth and small table in front of it to place my drinks. Ryan spots me when I come into his view.

"Hey, well, look who finally decided to show up," he yells over the noise in this place.

"Hey," I say, looking around to see if I know anyone at this table, and then I take a seat by one of his friends. A waitress comes up just as I sit down.

"I'll take a scotch on the rocks, please."

I look around the club. This place is busy tonight. I want to talk to Ryan about whatever he wants, and then I'm out of this place. I'm not looking for anyone tonight. I haven't been since my date with Emma. I think about her for a second, wondering what she is doing tonight, when Ryan interrupts my thoughts.

"Go out there and have some fun," he says as he points to the dance floor.

"No thanks, I'm only here because you wanted to talk."

Ryan gives me a frown, "Dave Riley said he hasn't heard from you in a couple of weeks. What's been going on with you? I thought you had this under control. We should've already closed this deal." he isn't happy with me.

We should have closed already, he's right, but his plan is a mess, and I don't want to do it anymore. I need a better plan, but I'm fresh out of ideas.

"Ryan, I can't do it. I can't drag Emma through this deal. We need to come up with a better plan." This is it, my confession I've been trying to avoid.

Ryan looks pissed, "there is no better plan, it's this or nothing. Want to be a billionaire or not" he shrugs and returns to his blonde.

I want the money, I do, and I want us to be the most successful real estate company in New York City but hurting someone along the way isn't something I want to do. I don't want to be that type of person anymore. Maybe meeting Emma showed me that I can be a better man.

I tip back my scotch and stare at the dance floor, knowing I should say goodbye to Ryan and get out of this place. We can deal with this shit on Monday. I spot a gorgeous blonde with her back turned to me dancing on the floor with a redhead and two men. The guys are all over the girls, who are way too good-looking for the guys dancing with them, but they look like they are having fun. The waitress interrupts my sight with a round of shots.

Ryan yells out, "Shots all around!"

We all stand, and each grabs a shot off the tray as the waitress passes it around. We all tap our shot glasses together in the air, then drop them back. When I put my shot glass back down on the tray, Ryan gets closer to me, points to the floor, and says, "Isn't that your girl over there?"

I look over to where he's pointing on the dance floor, and sure enough, the girls I just watched were Emma and Claire. My heart pounds into my chest, and I start sweating. What is she doing here? I hate myself for a minute for not talking to her and letting her go. She looks like she's having the time of her life, laughing and smiling while dancing with other guys. I start getting angry just watching someone else put their hands on her. The dark-haired guy has his hands on her waist while she is dancing with Claire. I can't help but think maybe she doesn't want him to touch her. Maybe she does.

That's it, it's time for me to go, but first, I need to do

something. I lean over into Ryan's ear to tell him I am leaving. He waves, and I tell him I'll see him on Monday. Then I make my way to where the girls are on the dance floor. She spots me when I get just a few feet away from Emma. Her one look gives me chills, and I can't help but smile back at her. She stops dancing, but everyone around her is still going. I walk straight up to the guy with his hands all over her. Then give him a straight punch right to the middle of his face.

"What the hell" the guy yells just as he grabs his face and falls over in pain.

Claire and the other guy give me a go-to-hell look, and then both help the guy I just punched in the face. It doesn't look good to me.

Emma gives me a shocked look. I nod at her, "Emma," and then head to the front door as quickly as possible.

I get to the door when I feel a hand grab my arm, the touch giving me a warm feeling.

"Baker, what the hell was that for"? Emma says as we walk out to the front of the club.

"He had his hands all over you" I turn to her, pissed off.

Emma stares off into the traffic. She looks mad, but I also can't help but think she is happy to see me. "Baker, you don't own me. I haven't heard from you in weeks. You can't do that... I can do whatever I want."

Ouch, I deserve that, but I'm also mad at myself for getting this far with someone. Emma's not wrong, she can do whatever she wants, but I don't want her to. Seeing her here brings back all those little new feelings I started feeling before I decided to end things. I kept telling myself it was what was best but was it?

I don't answer her and start walking down the sidewalk. I pull out my phone to text Carlos to have him get me around the corner of the club. I can hear her walking behind me when she shouts, "You aren't going to say anything? Fine then, ignore me. You seem to be good at that. I don't even know why I'm bothering trying to talk to you."

I hear her start to stop, then turn around to start heading back into the club. What the hell am I doing just letting her walk away? I turn around and run after her because what she said hurts, and I need to make it right with her.

"Emma, wait... stop. Let me explain," I catch up to her, grabbing her wrist before pulling her into my embrace. She's shaking and visibly upset with me.

I keep my arms wrapped around her.

"Look, I'm sorry..." I'm not good at this. I've never had to do this before. "I'm not sorry for punching that jerk who thought he could just touch you while dancing, that I can't take that back."

She starts crying, and now I feel like an ass again. This girl does a great job of making me feel like that. I hate seeing her upset, though. I give her a small kiss on the forehead. Then I pull her chin up with my hand so she can look me in the eyes.

"I am sorry, Em. I didn't mean to upset you. I don't even know what came over me in there. Seeing you with someone else hurts," I say as I wipe away the few tears she still has on her face. She then does the unexpected, she gets up on her toes, puts her hand behind my neck, bringing us closer, and then kisses me. It was a quick small kiss, but it gave me this overwhelming feeling. I cup her face with both hands on her cheeks and give her an even more significant, longer kiss back. I kiss her like I've missed her, longed for this moment since the last time I kissed her. I don't want this moment to end when she pulls away.

I need her, "Come with me."

She breaks our stares and looks down, "Baker, I can't...I

can't just leave Claire here. I came with her."

I forgot for a minute that she was here with Claire, I didn't want to leave her, but I understood that she probably didn't want to come with me considering what I'd done to her and tonight.

"Right…Can we talk later then?"

She takes a while to answer, just looking down

"Emma, please," I finally get her to look at me.

"I'll think about it. I need to head back now" Emma starts to turn around when I wrap my arms around her again in a tight hug.

"I'll make it up to you. Just text me later. Please," I let go of Emma, and she started heading back inside the club just as my driver pulled up to pick me up. I look back in her direction before getting into the car's back seat.

I have been tossing around my bed for what feels like hours. I can't get tonight out of my mind. I would have never expected to see Emma at Deuce. Seeing her brought back all these feelings I had bottled up for her. I need to see her again. I pick up my phone to see the time, and it's just after one am. I need to know that she at least made it home alright. I open our messages and start typing

Me: Just checking to make sure you made it home, okay?

I lay there for a minute, thinking maybe I shouldn't have texted her. Maybe she's still out. Maybe she doesn't even want to hear from me. A few minutes go by when I hear a ping

Emma: I made it home

Me: Well, goodnight, Em.

Emma: It was good seeing you, Baker, goodnight

Me: *blushing emoji

Emma: *middle finger emoji

What the hell!

Emma: OMG!! I didn't mean to send that. It was supposed to be the heart emoji.

Baker: Let's not send each other emojis anymore

Emma: Deal, you want to come over now?

She doesn't have to ask me twice. She sends me her apartment number, and it doesn't take me long to throw on some clothes and get out the door. I park outside her apartment building, making my way up to her apartment. She texts me that the front door is unlocked, so I go right in, locking the door behind me. I see a lamp in the back room, which must be her room. I get to her door just as she comes out of the bathroom. She's wearing just a t-shirt with some shorts, but somehow, she makes it look sexy.

She looks at me and smiles. "Hey."

I lean on the doorframe, nervous a little bit, but I still smile back, "Hey."

She goes around the bed, gets in, pulls the covers up, and then pats the spot next to her. I get to the other side of the bed, taking off my shoes before getting in with her. I'm not sure what our intentions are for the night.

She lays down on her side, with her head on her pillow facing me. I get under the covers and lay down facing her. We both smile at each other before I tell her to thank you for inviting me over.

"Claire would kill me if she knew you were over here. She's so mad at you for embarrassing her tonight."

"Well, let's just keep this our little secret," I laugh, but the thought of making her best friend mad doesn't sit well with me. I know many people hate me, but I don't want Claire to be one of them.

She is quiet for a second. I look at her and tuck a tiny piece of hair behind her ear while she stares at me. "I like you, Em." I don't even know where that came from. This woman makes me say and does things that I never had before.

"You scare me, Baker, we had a great time getting to know each other, and then I didn't hear from you for almost two weeks. I feel like there is a connection between us, but in my mind, I know we are different," she gives me a sad look.

"It wasn't my best move, just completely ghosting you. I shouldn't have done it, but I had a lot going on. I'll make it up to you" I scoot closer to her so we can cuddle. I put one arm over her while sliding the other under her neck so she could rest her head on it.

She gets comfortable. "How exactly are you going to make it up to me?"

I smile, "I'm not sure yet, but I'll figure it out."

"Can you promise me one thing?" she asks me sincerely.

"What's that"?

She puts her hand on my cheek, "Promise me that whatever this is between us, you will always be honest with me. I've had my heart broken for years now, and the only way I'll be able to open it up is with honesty. I need to know I can trust you."

"I promise, Em. You can trust me" Not knowing what the future holds for us, I can make this promise and enjoy this moment with her.

Chapter Six

Emma

I'm sitting at a table at The Brew House, waiting for Claire to join me. I sent her a text this morning asking her to meet me here to talk about last night. We left the club together, and once we got to our apartment building; we went our separate ways for the night. I want to let her know that Baker stayed with me last night. I can't lie to her about anything.

Just as I take a drink of my iced coffee, I hear the front door open and spot Claire making her way over to me. "Hey, Emma."

"Here, I got you a coffee," I slide her coffee across the table while she sits down.

"Thanks. What are you up to today?" Claire says just as she lifts her coffee to take a sip.

"Not much, really," I say, even though Baker was still in my bed when I left this morning. I woke him before I left. I wonder if he will still be there when I leave here.

She picks up her phone to check a message, then turns her attention back to me. "Sorry, I needed to get that" she doesn't mention who it was. "That's okay. I wanted to talk to you about something."

"What's up," she says, concerned. "You're my best friend, and I love you so much. You are the only person I can talk to about anything. I also don't want you to be mad at me, but I feel it's right to let you know that Baker stayed over last night."

She gasps, giving me a shocked look. "What! Emma, what he did last night was uncalled for."

"He did it because of me. He is sorry for it; he apologized many times last night to me. Claire, he doesn't want you to hate him. It was his idea for me to meet you first thing this morning to let you know he stayed, and he's sorry," I say, trying to justify that what he did was okay.

She's mad, "So it's alright to punch some random guy in the face because he put his hands on you."

"I didn't say it was Claire. I don't want you to be mad at Baker, I think he wants something with me, and he doesn't want you to be angry at him if we have something. We also didn't know those guys were at the club, anyway. Do you ever remember the guy's name?"

She stares at the back of the shop, thinking, "He will have to prove to me that he is good for you. I have waited years to be by your side while you date someone. You do need to be careful with him. We have never been around guys like him. we don't know what he could do. And you're right. I don't even remember that guy's name"

"We haven't made anything official, and we aren't exclusive just yet. He wants to make things right with you before we are. He knows that you are my family. You are everything to me."

She gives me a small smile, "I would have never thought you'd be the one to date a millionaire. I want one too."

I laugh, "He has a brother" I shrug at her and then get up from our small table. She gets up, too, blushing. "Oh, yes! Can't forget about him."

We embrace each other, then make our way out of the

coffee shop.

My apartment is empty when I get back, but I notice a note on the counter from Baker. I go to the counter to open the note he wrote on the back of an envelope.

Sorry I had to leave

Thank you for letting me stay and for the cuddles

I will talk to you later

Xo Baker

I don't have any plans today, so I'll get a few things around my apartment that I need to get done. I head into the bathroom to start the shower; I hit play music on my phone before getting in.

Shortly after getting ready, throwing on a cute yellow sundress with some white sneakers, I ran to the store to get a few things I needed for the week. I had called Claire to ask if she would want to come with me, but she said she needed a nap after last night's events. So, I decided to take off by myself.

The weather today couldn't be more perfect, a great day to take the long way to the store by walking through the park. The park is busy when I arrive, but since I'm walking through there today, I don't mind. I walk by many couples having picnics on blankets in the grass and make a mental note that I should ask Baker if he'd like to come to the park with me for lunch sometime. I think it would be great for him to appreciate something simple, something I would enjoy.

I'm making my way to the middle of the park. There's a large round fountain in the center of a massive walkway with benches to enjoy all views. I hear my phone go off in my purse, and I start searching all around my bag for my phone while I'm still walking when out of nowhere, a kid trying to catch a football falls right into me, knocking me down to the ground.

Luckily, I land on my bottom and save myself embarrassment from flashing everyone my goods in this dress. A shorter dark-haired older man runs over to me, "I'm so sorry. I didn't mean to throw the football your way." He puts his hand out to help me up from the ground. So, I give him my hand and get back on my feet, brushing my end with my hands to make sure I didn't land in anything. "Thank you for helping me up."

"It's no problem. I'm Dave," He puts his hand out to shake my hand.

"Hi, I'm Emma," I put my hand in his and gave him a slight shake.

"Emma Adler, owner of Blooms?" He looks at me as if he knows me.

"That would be me," giving him a puzzled look. I don't think I've ever been recognized in public before. How does he even know who I am, anyway?

"Well, Emma, sorry that my son here knocked you down. It was nice to meet you," he's smiling. "Let's hope he's learned his lesson and won't be knocking down any more pretty girls."

I blush, "It's alright... Well, it was nice to meet you guys. Hope you have a good day playing football,"

I go to walk away, and Dave says, "Nice to meet you too, Emma."

I finally fish my phone out of my bag. When I get a few seconds away from them, it's a text

Baker: Do you have any plans tonight?

Me: Walking to the store now. I can make you dinner.

Baker: Don't you own a car? Dinner sounds great, your place or mine.

Me: Mine, say around seven

Baker: See you then

If I owned a car like him, I'd probably drive all kinds of places, but Claire and I own a small car that only works when it wants to. Also, if I had driven, I probably wouldn't have had a silly accident like I did walking through the park today. I shouldn't tell him about it. He'll probably lecture me about how I should drive instead of walking. Maybe he would offer to let me drive his car next time, which I wouldn't mind.

I finally reach the grocery store. I grabbed the few needed things and tried to figure out what I should make for dinner. I know Baker likes Italian food, so I can't go wrong with making him some pasta. I get all the ingredients for a small homemade lasagna and grab a decent bottle of wine before reaching the checkout.

I have my reusable bags full of groceries in both my arms. I take a fast way home, avoiding the park, so I don't have to chance running into that guy again. I also don't want to carry these grocery bags very far. I'm not into working out at the expensive workout classes here in New York City, so I choose to be a wimp.

I round the corner to my apartment building, and there stands Baker waiting for me by the front entrance, looking tall, dark, and handsome with his dark hair and green eyes, wearing dry-fit shorts with a t-shirt, looking like he just came from the gym. Once he spots me, he runs up to me, taking my bags. "Let me take those." I am all surprised to see him because I am.

"I said seven," handing him over the bags in my arms.

Taking the grocery bags in his hands, he walks beside me

as we make our way inside. "When you said you walked, I knew you'd need help carrying the bags up the steps."

"Well, thank you for coming to my rescue. My arms were starting to fall off little by little." I giggle as we make our way up the staircase. My apartment building isn't fancy enough to have an elevator.

"If you aren't going to drive, next time, I will take you," Baker says as we make it to my door. I take the keys from my purse to unlock it and make our way into my tiny apartment. He goes over to the counter to set down the bags, and I follow behind so that I can unload their bags. "that's kind of you, but I didn't mind walking on a nice day like today."

I finish unloading the first bag when he spots a small scrape on my forearm, "What happened here?"

I look over to the spot he pointed at my arm; from when I fell in the park, I must have gotten the scrape but didn't notice. "I might have had a small run-in with a little boy in the park. I was trying to get my phone out of my purse when a little boy ran into me while playing football with his dad. The man helped me up. It wasn't that big of a deal."

"Geez, Emma, you need to be careful when walking," he grabs a towel, wets it, then wipes off the scrape.

"It wasn't exactly my fault. The guy apologized for his son knocking me over. The guy was strange, though. He knew who I was, but I didn't think I had ever met him. I think he said his name was David or something like that."

"Hmmm... Maybe from the paper?" Baker says while he finishes cleaning the tiny scratch.

"Maybe"

I'm starting dinner early since Baker never left my apartment after assisting me with my groceries. I start assembling the lasagna while Baker pours us a couple of glasses of wine. "Can you tell me what your parents were like?" he asks unexpectedly.

I give him a frown, "They were the best parents. They were high school sweethearts who got married right out of college. I don't think I've ever seen two people more in love with each other. I would walk into the kitchen in the mornings and see them slowly dancing while drinking coffee. It is one memory of them that I'll never forget. They were always happy and were friends with everyone back home. I hated to leave them, but they supported me through everything I wanted to do with my life," I answer as I finish putting the cheese on top of the lasagna and throw it in the oven.

He sets his glass of wine down on the counter, "My parents met right before college but had my sister while they were in their third year of college. My mother dropped out to stay home while my dad went on to finish law school, becoming a lawyer so he could support us. My parents are probably the opposite of yours, my mother is great and has always supported us through everything, but my father was strict, always hard on us."

"You have a sister. How fun. I always wanted a sister" I go to sit by him at the bar while we wait for dinner.

"You will have to meet her soon. She is married with two children. We make family dinners at my parents once a month. I will have to bring you to one of them sometime" he pauses for a moment.

"Why didn't your parents have any more children"? Our conversation is turning into a serious one.

"My parents tried for years after they had me to have one more, and it never happened. They were pleased with me, but I could tell they always wanted to give me a sibling. Claire and I met in grade school, so she was essentially my sister growing up" I don't tell him that I'm worried about going to meet his parents and family. I haven't been to a large family gathering since before my parents passed, and the thought makes me sad.

He turns towards me, resting his hand on my thigh while I continue to drink my wine. The wine I bought may be cheaper than what he buys, but he doesn't seem to mind. He picks his glass up, smiling at me before taking a sip. I smile back, "What are you smiling about?"

Sitting his glass back on the counter, "You talk much more when you're home or at my place. Is there a reason for that?"

"I'm not sure if you know what it means, but I'm an Enneagram nine. Being comfy and at home is my comfort. Homebody is my middle name" I let out a giggle. "I like simple things, reading a book on the couch with a blanket, enjoying walks in the park. I guess you could say I am an easygoing person."

"I know what it is, I went to a conference for work once, and they had us take a test to figure out our number, so we could better understand ourselves. My number is obvious, and I'm a three. I'm a go-getter, workaholic, competitive, holds in my emotion, overachiever, but I have great people skills," he smirks.

"I haven't studied numbers beside a nine, but I would say those qualities describe you." I get up from my chair and head to the fridge to take everything out to make a salad.

"I think a nine and a three would work well together. You can be encouraging, while I can offer you confidence. You can teach me to slow down, and we will look at the positives in life." he says, following me to the fridge. I start handing him things as

I pull them out, and he sets them on the counter.

"You did study this stuff," I say as I grab a cutting board from the upper cabinet.

"I did, and I think I better understand the person you are now that I know your number. I would say you should check out the enneagram hive on Instagram, but you don't have social media" he looks embarrassed, like he didn't mean to admit he might have looked me up.

"About that ... I do, but I just might have prevented you from being able to find me. It's something I did the day after our little one-night stand instinctively. I didn't want you to find out much about me. It's not like there's much on there anyways. My life isn't that interesting."

"You know you shouldn't call it a one-night stand anymore. How about we call that night..." he leans up against the counter, placing his finger on his chin to think for a second, "we should call it our secret meeting."

I'm so confused, "Secret Meeting?"

"Yea, it sounds better... We can call it that since no one knows about it but us. No one needs to know about it anyways, plus we made a deal that we wouldn't do something like that again unless it. Means something, so that night is behind us now."

"Well, Claire knows about it, but she wouldn't say anything... So, we will call it our secret meeting, and we never have to talk about it again, but we can still think about it."

"Exactly. And trust me, I still think about it," Baker says with a smile.

I blush because I still think about that night too. *All the time*

We just finished up eating dinner. Baker picks up both of our plates and heads to the kitchen sink. “You cooked, so I’ll clean up.”

I get up, pick the wine glasses off my tiny dining table and meet him at the sink, “I can’t let you do that; this is my home, so I can help you clean.”

“Thank you for having me over for dinner. You’ll make me solid if you always feed me like this.” He rinses off some of the dishes, handing them to me to place into the dishwasher.

“Well, I can’t cook much, so don’t worry, your precious babies” I run my hand across his abs. “Will not be going anywhere.”

“Meet me at the gym tomorrow after you close up for the day,” he gives me a severe look. “We could work out together, and I can show you how I get these abs.”

“I’m not sure that’s a good idea. I haven’t been to a gym, ever.” I bite down on my bottom lip nervously.

“You’ll be in good hands; I won’t let anything happen to you,” he says in a clear tone.

I think about it for a minute. I seriously haven’t worked out a day in my life. I’ve never even stepped foot into a gym, so of course, I say, “I guess I’ll come,” but I’m pretty sure I will embarrass myself.

He pulls me into his arms, giving me a hold. “Thank you for giving me a second chance. Tonight, with you, was perfect, and I can’t wait for many more nights like these”

“You know how to make a girl feel special” I smile at him.

He lets go of me and crosses his arms across his chest. “I

hate to say it, but I have to head home. I have a few things I need to get done before work tomorrow."

"I'll see you tomorrow after work, then."

I follow him to my front door; he turns to me, and I think he's going to kiss me goodbye, but he says, "Yes, tomorrow… Bye, Em," and then he walks out the door.

Chapter Seven

Baker

I pull up outside the office on Monday morning, I usually wouldn't say I like this place on Mondays, but I have something to look forward to at the end of this workday for once. I'm not sure what came over me to invite her to the gym, but I just thought maybe she would like to do something I like to do. Yesterday with her was just what I needed, getting to know her better.

I shut the car door on my Range Rover, and I drive this car more, knowing it's her favorite. I walk through the office's two big glass front doors and, once in, greeting by my assistant, Marie. "Hello, Mr. Hayes. You don't have any phone calls this morning. I put your mail on your desk. If you need anything today, just let me know." I acknowledge her with a nod, making my way to my office. "Thank you, Marie."

I get into my office, which is furnished with a large black desk and two caramel-colored leather chairs. It has a wall of glass, which has to pull down shades for days. I need privacy. Today being one of those, I close the shades but open the curtains to the windows overlooking the city. I sit in my office chair behind my desk, sorting through the mail. I notice an invitation from the city, most likely for their annual charity event.

I open the invitation,

You're formally invited to the 52nd annual Charity Gala for the businesses of New York City, and this event is on August 27th at 7 pm. It will take place at the Windsor Ballroom, owned by the wonderful Baker and Ryan Hayes. All money raised at this year's event will be donated to local Children's Hospitals.

Taking the invitation, I pin it up on my board with other invitations to past events I haven't taken down. I wonder if Emma and Claire got one. I can't recall seeing them there in past years, but it would be great for them if they want to expand their business. I'll have to get with the head of the event to make sure they send them an invite. I can't help but think this would be a great event to make it official with Emma and let everyone know of our relationship, and I know Dave Riley will be there. I'm not using Emma to seal the deal with him, but I want him to know that I've cleaned up my womanizing act.

I open my schedule on the computer to see what I need to do for the day. I have a couple of showings for some new business opportunities. I see that I have a note to call Dave Riley today. Ryan must have added that to my schedule himself. I pull my phone out, and just as I check my messages, Ryan comes through my office door.

"Hey, just checking on you today. I haven't seen you since the other night at the club" he takes a seat in one of the chairs in my office.

"Don't you know how to knock...Sorry, I was busy. What's up? You need something?" I don't even make eye contact with him and keep going through my phone.

"You going to call Dave today." He sounds angry.

"Yes," sounding annoyed, I finally look up at him.

"I was wondering. Dave hasn't heard from you in a while. Tell him you're seeing someone. Maybe we can close it after the gala. That is a month away, which is the perfect time to close. We can spend the winter months putting businesses in the buildings, and by this time next year, we will be billionaires spending the summers on a yacht in Santorini, Greece" he sounds ludicrous. His life plans are much different than mine.

"You go do that while I stay here taking care of all our business. It would help if you grew up, Ryan. I want these buildings, but I don't plan on spending my earnings on yachts and vacations. I want to build this business so that maybe one day when I finally settle down, I'll have someone to pass this business down to for generations. Money doesn't mean as much to me as it does to you. You do stupid shit with your money. So, let me handle this while you figure out how to be a man."

I understand that he is my brother, and I love him, but I need him to become more responsible. I built this business for us while he sat back, enjoying the ride. I'm going to need him. If we get these buildings, we will have our hands full, and I can't do all the work myself.

I know he's angry with me. "Just finish this, okay."

"Got it, now you can leave" I don't even watch him leave; I get right back to checking my phone.

Once he leaves, shutting the door behind him. I open my text with Emma

Me: Are we still on for today?

I send it, then hit call on Dave Riley's number, and he answers after the second ring.

"Hey Dave, how are you doing today?"

"Well, if it isn't Baker Hayes, what's it been? Hasn't it been three weeks since I last heard from you? How are you doing?"

"I've been great, Dave; I have had a lot going on lately. Have you been enjoying the summer with the family?"

"I sure have. The kids and I have been staying busy. Will I see you at this year's Charity event at the end of the summer?"

"You sure will, Dave. You know I wouldn't miss it for the world."

"You have anyone special to bring as your date?"

"I do. You will have to meet her then."

"Well, that is good to hear. I'm sure she is lovely. I'll see you there, if not before then."

"Sounds good, Dave, Have a great rest of the summer."

This call was just a check-in with him, letting him know we are still on his radar but not begging him to sell the buildings to us now. I hang up, setting my phone on my desk. That was one of the more effortless conversations I have had with Dave. I want to build trust with him and prove we want them for the right reasons before we try to seal the deal. If I let Ryan do this, he would go about it the wrong way, and we would've already lost them to someone else, which is why I put a stop to Ryan's idea of how to get in better with Dave. I'll take care of this my way, and that's just earning his trust.

I finished up a few meetings at some of the buildings we have open now. It's been a long day, and I still haven't heard back from Emma. She could be busy today since she and Claire run the shop themselves with no other employees but delivery drivers. I'm not far from their shop, so I pick them up some lunch, maybe earning a few bonus points from Claire, and drop it off to them.

I stopped in the Sandwich Shop and picked them up a couple of salads and some water. Then, I make my way over to their shop just a few doors down. I open the front door, and right when I get inside, I see Claire pop her head around a huge flower arrangement, “Hello.”

“Hey, I brought you two some lunch. Emma here?” I hold up the bag of food to show her.

“You are so kind. We are starving. Emma is in the back putting in an order. You can take lunch back there. Thanks for bringing us something.”

“It’s no problem,” I say as I head to the back office.

I remember where the office was from the last time I was there. When I reach the doorway, Emma spots me, sporting a huge grin. She’s wearing just a t-shirt, jeans, and a messy bun, an effortless look, but I like it. I can’t help but smile at her back. “You didn’t respond to my text, so I figured you were busy. Brought you two some lunch.”

“You text me? I’m so sorry. I keep my phone in my bag when I am here. Thanks for lunch. You didn’t have to do that.”

I take a seat across from her, “Actually, I did,” I point out in the direction of Claire. “I figured I could warm her back up to me by bringing her food.”

She laughs. “Of course, you would think of that.”

She took the salad and water out of the bag I brought and opened the cap on the water to take a drink. “So, are we still on for tonight after work?”

“Oh yes, the gym” she takes the lid off the salad to mix it around and takes a bite

“We can get in a little cardio,” I watch her as she eats so gracefully.

“You know, that sounds exhausting, but I can at least try. Just to put a smile on your face,” Emma looks at me as she takes another bite of her salad.

"Good. What time do you close up today?"

"We close at six. I can meet you there around six thirty," Emma doesn't take her eyes off me while she eats, which is kind of sexy.

I get up from the chair, "I hope you enjoyed your lunch. I'll see you in a few hours, okay."

"Okay. Thanks again, Baker."

"Anytime" I walk out of the office and wave Claire goodbye before heading out the front door. I've never brought a woman lunch at her work before, but this somehow feels normal bringing her lunch.

I get into my car, heading back to my office to finish the last things I had on my schedule for the day. I quickly call the Charity gala event coordinator to ensure they send Emma and Claire an invite. I know it's just the thing they need to boost their plans to get a more extensive shop.

I look over at the clock on my office desk, which reads 6:00. I didn't realize the time had gone by fast the last few hours. I have my gym bag resting in my chair, so I can change it here before leaving, so I have a couple more minutes to finish up. I was closing out of tomorrow's schedule when I got a text from Emma saying she may be a few minutes late. They had a couple of last-minute orders come in. I decide I'll get a head start at the gym while waiting for her. I change my gym clothes, then get into my car to head for the gym.

When I get into the gym, with a couple of water bottles just in case Emma forgot one. It's now 6:25, so I have some time to warm up on the treadmill before she gets here. I get a good pace when I start feeling eyes on me from across the room. I turn around to notice that the person staring me down is Madison, a "not so real" blonde with whom I have a past. I took her out once, maybe slept with her, and then she went psycho-crazy and started obsessing over me. She's not exactly a person I want to run into out in public, especially if Emma is meeting me here. I pretend like I didn't see her and, for a minute, contemplate just telling Em we can skip the gym tonight, but we've already had this planned.

I've been on the treadmill for about twenty minutes when I spot a hot blonde coming my way wearing a white sports bra, navy athletic leggings, and white tennis shoes, and I can't help but get a smile on my face while she makes her way over. I stop the treadmill, get down and greet her with a bear hug. Maybe I should take her back to her place dressed like this and forget working out.

"Well, are you ready for this? I'll try not to embarrass you" she bites down on her bottom lip like she's nervous.

"You get on this treadmill by me, and we can start at a jog" I help her up on the treadmill, then show her the settings. "I'm going to start you out at a low number, and if you can handle more, press the higher number for it to go quicker. Got it"

"Got it" I press the three, knowing it's the best number to start.

I returned to the pace I had set for myself before she showed up. "How was work today?"

She seems to be doing well. I'm impressed. "It was good, busy."

"Busy is good...How are you holding up over there?"

"I'm fine. It isn't so bad."

And just as she answers my question, Madison comes over to the treadmill on the other side of me and starts jogging at a quick pace. I try not to notice her because I don't want her to cause a scene in front of Emma.

We have all been jogging next to each other for an eternity. It's only been a few minutes.

Emma looks over to me, noticing Madison on the other side. Then I see Emma press the number four so she can go at a faster pace. I know what Emma's trying to do. She's trying to keep up with Madison.

She seems to be doing well now, but I know she will start wearing down soon. We all go at the same pace for another 10 minutes. I'm still doing my best not to pay attention to Madison next to me, so Emma doesn't think I'm checking her out or giving her the slightest hint that I may know her.

Just out of my eye, I see Madison going faster. I think, please don't even try Emma, please don't. She looks over at me, and I shake my head no, but she doesn't notice. She pushes the next level and acts like she's been running her whole life when I know she's probably dying inside during this moment because I know I am. It is not how I wanted this night to go. I close my eyes and think this will not turn out well.

Emma is going strong, and I think she's ready to be my running partner. We don't even need these gym sessions anymore. We should get off these things right now, leave, and I could get away from whatever is about to happen here. I mean, waxing my private area sounds more pleasing than this situation I have going on right now. I am still holding on to not noticing Madison. I think she will give up on this little act she has going on.

I can see Madison, out of my eye, push a button on her treadmill, and it starts to slow down and then completely stops. I feel like I am finally going to get out of this mess. Still, when I think this foolishness is finally coming to an end, Madison walks straight over to me, smacks my ass as hard as she can while I'm running, and says, "I've missed you" I am shaking at this moment, like did that happen. But I quickly snapped out of it when I heard a loud gasp. I look over to see Emma's appalled face, and then she stops running, the treadmill throwing her back where she falls straight on her ass, and her head falls back to the ground. *Shit.*

I shut my treadmill off as quickly as possible and ran to Emma. She's on the ground with her hands over her face. "Are you okay? I'm so sorry." I put my hand out to help pull her up off the floor. She doesn't even acknowledge me standing there, clearly embarrassed. She has her hands over her face, lying there for another eternity. When I saw Madison was here, I knew I should've changed our plans and left. Lesson learned, never bringing Emma back to the gym was my fault, not hers.

Emma finally takes her hands off her face and puts her hand in mine so I can pull her up. She doesn't say anything.

"I already know the answer but want to get out of here?"

"Please, I think I've embarrassed myself enough for today."

We get in my car, and we both sit there in silence. Emma heard what she said when she touched me, but she probably didn't want to talk about it. "You want to get some food, go home, or we can go to my place? What sounds better to you?"

She doesn't answer and bites down on her bottom lip like she was doing earlier when she was nervous. "Can you stop doing that with your lip? It tells me what to do to you" I'm trying anything to cheer her up. She finally looks my way, "Can we get cheeseburgers? I always want carbs when I'm stressed."

"Cheeseburgers when you are stressed, note taken, but yes," I smile at her and then reach over to take her hand in mine.

We walk through her apartment door with burgers, fries, and sodas in hand, food I don't usually eat but I'll do for her. I don't think I have even been with a girl who doesn't care what kind of food she eats. When we were in the drive-thru to order food, Emma wanted to order everything on the menu, and I was going to let her. We sit on her couch, and she's already grabbed her fries out of the bag, stuffing them in her mouth like she's starving. She flips on the TV, turning it to an episode of Schitt's Creek. "This okay with you? I've seen this show a hundred times so that I can turn it."

I was impressed with her choice of a tv show, "Who doesn't love Eugene Levy? This is one of my favorites. We can watch this."

She pulls the rest of our food out of the bag, handing me my fries. "So, do you want to tell me who she is? Not that it matters or anything, I just wanted to know," she sits down cross-legged on the couch to get comfy.

"She's someone I went out with once. She meant nothing to me. She was crazy, and I ended up having to block her from my phone and work calls" I turned toward her while I talked to her.

She doesn't seem bothered by what I told her about Madison.

"So, you slept with her"

I give her a serious look because she wants me to be honest, and I want her to trust me, "I did. One time, not that, that makes it sounds better". She turns towards the tv, opens the wrapper from her burger, and then takes a huge bite. I decide to do the same. She then blurts out, "I am so annoyed at myself for trying to race her on the treadmill. She's like way hotter and in better shape, than I am. I don't know what I was thinking?"

"Woah, Woah" I tap her leg with my hand, and her turning towards me. "You are way hotter than her. I thought your little competitive attitude was incredibly sexy. Also, never compare yourself to anyone else" I can't help but look into her bright green eyes when I talk to her. She scoots closer, so her crossed legs are touching my leg. She leans over to the coffee table, sets her food down quickly, and then gives all her attention back to me. “Well, I thought it was extremely hot that someone else was trying to hit on you in front of me at the gym, but I’m not sure I want to go back there.”

“Not going back there. Your little competition was enough to prove to me you can be my running partner” I give her a laugh.

“Does that mean you’re going to call me at 5 am on a Saturday to run the streets because I like my bed that early in the morning” she gives me a fake frown and then smiles?

“I like to go whenever I need to clear my head which can be any time of the day” I rest my hand on her leg. I have never been one for physical touch, but with her, it's comfortable.

“You want to stay tonight?” she smiles sweetly.

“How about you pack an overnight bag, and we can stay at my place tonight?” giving her the same smile. She gets up from the couch, yelling “Deal” as she walks down the hall to her bedroom.

Waking up before my alarm goes off to Emma’s head resting on my chest, her arm across my body. She has this fruity smell to her, and I like it. I take my arm off her back to rub my eyes so I can wake up. This feeling of waking up to her is one of the perfect feelings; I instantly get a smile. I slowly get up from the bed, sliding her off me carefully, so I don’t wake her. We have not been intimate since the first night we met, which is one of the best things about our relationship. It would typically bother me to have her stay over to sleep, but with her, it's different than women from my past. She’s different. Emma is not the girl you have sex with, and if I had known more about her the night, we probably wouldn’t have done it then.

I go down the stairs to the kitchen, starting a pot of coffee to take some with us on our way to work. I go back upstairs to get in the shower. When I reach the room, I cannot help but watch her sleep peacefully and comfortably in my bed. I have this ache in my chest that I could watch her sleep like this every morning. I brush my fingers over her forehead, moving her hair off her face. She wiggles just a little from my touch and then opens her eyes.

I whisper, "Good Morning" she smiles and then moans while she stretches out. "Good morning. What time is it?"

"It's early. Go back to sleep, and I'll wake you when it's time for you to get up," I say, and Emma falls asleep before I get into the shower.

I walk into my closet once I'm out of the shower to get dressed for the day when I notice her bag sitting on the large bench I have in the middle of my closet. She has her outfit for the day hanging in the empty side of the closet. An idea comes to me, and I hope she loves surprises.

When I walk out of the closet to the bedroom, she's coming into the room with a cup of coffee in her hand, "wow, you look nice," she says before taking a drink of her coffee.

"I didn't even hear you wake up. Are you already having coffee"? She walks into the bathroom while talking, "I like my coffee right out of bed."

"Good to know. We can leave after you get ready. I'll be in the kitchen waiting" I make my way downstairs. I sit at the kitchen island, opening my laptop that I always keep here. I emailed someone to help me with my surprise for Emma and then grabbed some coffee. I've been downstairs for fifteen minutes when Emma is dressing to leave and to walk down the stairs.

"You're done already?" I say, watching her come down the stairs dressed in the jeans and T-shirt she had hanging in the closet with sneakers, her hair in a ponytail.

"I just took a quick rinse and then got dressed. It wasn't hair washing day."

I look at her confused, "Wait, you only have certain days to wash your hair."

She comes over to pour more coffee into her cup, "Washing my hair every day is a chore, so I only wash it every other day. You wouldn't understand."

"Well, I'm learning new things about you this morning. I guess we can be early today. You have everything you need"?

She picks up her bag off the entryway table and puts it on her shoulder, "I sure do."

We pull up outside Blooms, and I notice the billboard out front. I guess I've never really paid much attention when stopping by here. "You do have to look at me every day" Remembering what she said the first night I met her. She looks out the window and then back at me. "At first, I hated it, but I guess it's growing on me now," she laughs.

"Will you keep your phone on you, just in case I need to hear from you?" She puts her hand on the handle to open the door, "I will try my best. Have a great day," as she opens the door to the car. "You too, Em," I say as I watch her get out, close the door, and then walk to the front door. I stay just a minute longer, ensuring she unlocks the door and makes her way inside. When she does, she turns to wave, and I wave back before I drive off.

Chapter Eight

Emma

"You've been rather cheery today. Could It have anything it does with a certain guy" Claire says to me as she's sweeping the shop floor? We are closing for the day. I'm waiting for her to finish so we can walk to the apartment building together.

"Maybe... Things with us have been going well since he came over the night after the club incident. I like him," I sit on the stool at the front counter.

"Who wouldn't fall for a rich guy," she continues sweeping.

I have my elbows on the counter, resting my head on my hands, "It's not like that with him, though. You would never guess he has money; everything seems effortless with him, and our conversations seem natural."

"I'm happy for you, Emma, I am," she's finishing sweeping and now heading to the back to put the broom up.

I get up from the front counter to follow her. "Thank you, Claire means a lot to me."

I kept my phone in my apron today, getting messages throughout the day from Baker. He said he was busy with something tonight, so he wouldn't be able to see me and told me to have some girl time with Claire. He said he had a surprise for me Thursday night and would see me then. I'm not even sure what surprise he could have for me.

On the way to our apartments, Claire and I decided we would have a girls' night at her place. When we arrived, we ordered some pizza to be delivered, and they poured us a couple of glasses of wine.

"Your place looks great. I haven't been here in what, a year," I'm walking around with my wine in my hand.

"I don't think you've been since before, James. We always went to your apartment because he never wanted you over."

I roll my eyes, "Oh, James...I'm glad we don't have to worry about that guy anymore."

Claire sits on the couch with her wine glass, "I can't believe I let him stick around for as long as I did."

I take a seat by her on her little yellow sofa. Claire's apartment is very colorful, which fits perfectly with her personality. We hardly ever fight about anything because we balance each other well. She is fearless, while I can be reserved.

"So, you want to watch something?" I ask her.

"Sure, you pick. I'm getting bored of picking my tv shows to watch. I sometimes click through Netflix for an hour and then shut the tv off." I laugh because that sounds like Claire. I turn the tv on, only to click on where we left off, watching The Golden Girls the other night. We have watched this show for years and still enjoy all the episodes.

"So, I've been meaning to ask you. The night when we left the bar with Baker and Ryan, what did you and Ryan do after you two left?" I turn to her, hoping she has something exciting to say.

"So that night after Ryan and I left the bar, he brought

me home. I told you this already. We exchanged numbers, and occasionally, he texts me for advice about women."

"What. That's a total jerk move. Why would Ryan need you to give him advice? He doesn't need your advice about getting girls. He gets them without it. I wonder if he has different motives for texting you," There must be a reason why he is texting her for advice, or maybe that's just what Claire is telling me. She could be hiding something.

She takes a while to say anything, and when she finally opens her mouth to say something, we hear a knock on the door. Claire gets up from the couch to answer the door. It's the pizza delivery guy. She tips the delivery guy before grabbing the pizza and then shuts the door.

"Pizza is here! Let's eat!" she goes to the kitchen to set the pizza on the kitchen island.

We spend the rest of the night at her place, eating and watching tv, and we never bring up the Ryan situation again, but she does ask some questions about Baker, and that's when I tell her the dreaded story of the gym. Then she spends the rest of the night making fun of me, for you guessed it, running.

It isn't too late when I get back to my apartment. I shower, wash my hair, and then throw on some clothes to sleep in. It's quiet here, and after sleeping at Baker's place last night, I'm not sure I like sleeping alone anymore. Maybe I should have stayed at Claire's for the next few nights since I won't see him again till Thursday. It's been a few hours since I last heard from him, and I wonder what he's been doing. Instead of texting like we usually do, I call him instead. It only rings once before he answers. "Hey"

He sounds happy to hear from me, "Hey, what are you doing?"

"I just got out of the shower; I'm going to bed soon, but I wanted to hear from you before I fell asleep," I say as I'm lying across my bed, staring at the ceiling.

"Was it a hair-washing shower?" I can tell he's smiling.

I laugh, "Yes, it was."

"Did you have a good night with Claire?"

"We just ordered some pizza and watched tv at her place for a couple of hours, but it was a nice time."

"That's good. Did you call because you missed me?"

I smile, "Maybe, my home is just so quiet."

I can tell he's smiling, too, "Just one more night. It will be worth it, I promise."

"I hope so... Goodnight, Baker" I don't want to get off the phone, but it's late.

"Goodnight, Em"

I hang up the phone, laying there for a moment longer. I feel like I'm falling for Baker, but I still need to be careful. It's all happening too fast.

It's finally Thursday, and I am halfway through the workday at the Flower shop. Claire and I haven't stopped once today. We have been getting so much business that I'm beginning to think that perhaps we should hire one more florist to catch a break.

Last night I went home after work, ate a bag of chips for dinner, and went to bed early because even though I've done that routine for the last five years, I don't like it anymore, and I'm ready to spend more nights with Baker. He has already been in touch with me today, telling me he was picking me up from work tonight. I'm grateful we have been busy, so this day should go by quickly.

"So, you still don't know what the surprise is?" Claire asked while we were both working on bouquets with several different types of flowers.

"Not a clue," staying focused on the arrangement I have been working on. I hear the door open and see the mailman bringing in the mail. He walks over to the front counter setting the mail down, "There you go, ladies, have a great day," he says as he walks back to the front door.

"Thank you"

I finish up, and then I stick the arrangement in the cooler until the delivery driver shows up for more deliveries.

I go to the front counter to grab our mail so that I can place it in the office.

I notice the top mail is a fancy envelope from the city.

When I get to the office, I open it,

"You're formally invited to the 52nd annual Charity Gala for the businesses of New York City. This event is on August 27th at 7 pm. It will take place at the Windsor Ballroom, owned by the wonderful Baker and Ryan Hayes. All money raised at this year's event will be donated to local Children's Hospitals."

What. I can't believe we finally got an invitation. I walk out of the office and yell to Claire, "You won't believe this. We got invited to the Charity Gala."

She squeals while jumping up and down. "Seriously!"

Even though I know Baker had something to do with this, I'm thankful he invited us. We have been trying to get an invitation for all five years we have been in business here. It is an event to help us get our name out there for people who don't know about us. We will have to consider what we want to donate for them to auction off.

"Yes, I'm sure Baker had some part in this, but I am so excited that we will finally be able to put our business out there."

"You owe him big time for this," she laughs. I roll my eyes because I'm sure she means something dirty. I make my way back into the office, hanging the invitation on the wall cardholder we keep.

Cleaning the counters while Claire sweeps the floors like she always does. "You promise you'll text me later to let me know how tonight went, right."

I pay attention to cleaning, not looking at her. "I promise, if you don't hear from me, you will find out first thing in the morning."

I hear a knock on the front door when I finish wiping the front counter, and when I look up, I see Baker at the door, dressed like he just came from work. I go over to open the door for him, "Hey," I say when he walks in.

"Are you finished? I can wait," before I can even say anything, Claire says, "She's all done. She can go," sending Claire a thank you look, "Since I finished, we can go now."

When we got to the car, he opened the door for me. Laying across the passenger seat is a giant bouquet, an arrangement that looks familiar. I clearly remember Claire putting them together today, and I observed her the whole time, thinking it was the loveliest mix of flowers she had ever made. My heart flutters. "Seriously," I say.

Baker answers, "I asked Claire to make these, and then she sent them to my office."

"Baker, I love them, thank you...She's in trouble" I pick the flowers up and then get in the car.

He gets in on the other side and closes his door, "She may have gotten a little extra for keeping the secret" he reaches for my hand and take mine into his.

"So where are we going?" I ask while looking out the side window while he drives.

"We are going to my place" he squeezes my hand, brushing his thumb over my knuckles.

It felt like a longer-than-normal drive to get here, but dinner was waiting for us on the kitchen island when we finally made it to his apartment. He got pasta from the place we had our first official date. "I ordered in because I know how comfortable you are just being at home" there's something about how he just said home.

"Thank you, but you didn't have to do that. What exactly is the special occasion?" I ask, walking over to the kitchen and setting the flowers in the island's center.

"You will have to wait. Let's eat first," Baker says, getting our plates ready.

I sit next to him on the island, "So I take it you missed me the last couple of days."

He's pouring us wine, the same kind we had the night we ate at the restaurant, "Maybe just a little," he says jokingly. I give him a little push of his arm, and he says, "I missed you a lot."

"That's good because I missed you a lot too."

We have been eating dinner and discussing work for the last few days. Baker seems to be just as busy as I am during the days. We both finished eating quickly, I skipped lunch, so I was starving. He always gives me an impressive look when he sees how much food I can put down.

I assisted him with cleaning up our dinner mess, even though he told me he didn't want help. I enjoy it when we do these sorts of things together. Once we finish, he takes my hand, "I want to show you something," displaying the most radiant grin on his face.

"Okay" I follow him up the stairs while he still has my hand in his. When we get to the bedroom door, it's shut. He turns to me, "Are you ready for your surprise?"

"Are you about to get naked? I wouldn't consider that a surprise. I've seen you naked before," he laughs, "Em, it's not me naked... Come on," he turns around to open the door, my hand still in his.

When I walked into the room, I was amazed that he had changed the room. Instead of the masculine touches it once had, it's now a neutral-colored room with a gray upholstered headboard, all-white bedding, navy blue throw pillows, and a gray blanket over the end of the bed. He replaced the once dark wood nightstands with black ones for both sides of the bed and white lamps for each nightstand.

My jaw drops, "Wow...Baker, this looks incredible."

"Isn't it great? I hired an interior designer to come help renovate the room. I want this to feel like home for you." I am surprised. It was not what I expected from him. We haven't seen each other for very long.

"I don't know what to say," I say because I have no words.

He pulls me towards the bathroom, "one more thing."

"Because I feel like this is already enough" we get to the closet door, which is also closed.

He turns to me with a giant smile on his face. "I saved the best for last," and then he opens the door.

The once-dark closet is now all white, with a square blush-colored ottoman in the middle and a huge crystal chandelier hanging from the middle of the ceiling. The closet that was once full of his clothes is now wall-to-wall full of women's clothing of all types and shoes. I can't believe my eyes; this closet is an absolute dream. It can't possibly be for me. He's still standing in the closet doorway with his hands in his pockets, watching me as I look around at everything. "What do you think?"

"I love it," I wave my hand around, "This is all for me? How did you even know my size?" I turn to him, and he makes his way over to me.

"It's all yours, and I had a personal shopper get all these clothes. I gave him your size, which I looked at when your clothes were here the other day, and told him what clothes you typically wear. I want you to have your own space here. I want you to come here and feel at home. All these clothes are so you don't have to pack a bag, you can stay anytime you want. It is what has kept me busy the last two days. When you stayed the other night, I knew I would want you to stay whenever you wanted, so I knew what I wanted to do. There's something else I want to show you."

I don't think there is anything else he can do to make this moment better when he walks over to a row of t-shirts hanging on one of the walls and pulls out a blush pink shirt that says Blooms Flowers across the front, "I had a local company make shirts for you and Claire for work."

I can't hold back anymore. I shed a single tear. "Baker, I love this so much. You didn't have to do this. I'm so sorry. These are happy tears."

He comes over to me, wrapping his arms around me, "Claire loves them too. I sent her over a box today."

"What, she knows about these" I pull out of his arms to look up at him. "Well, I needed someone to help me pick out what they should look like."

"I don't know how I'll ever be able to pay you back for this."

"You don't have to; this is my gift to you... So, you're staying tonight?"

I laugh, "of course, I am," I almost wanted to say I'm staying forever, but forever may be too long for Baker Hayes.

I get on actual pajamas to sleep in. I've slept in t-shirts and cotton shorts for as long as I can remember, but there are actual pajama sets in my new closet. There are also matching lingerie sets that I'll gladly save for another night. Baker was already in bed, just waiting for me to join him, but I promised Claire I would text her. Not surprised she already knew what the real surprise was. I can't believe she was able to keep it from me.

While going through the whole closet, looking for something to sleep in, I texted Claire. I sent her a few pictures of the costly clothes in the closet before finally settling on a navy-blue matching set of soft fabric shorts with a tank top to sleep in for the night.

I turn off all the bathroom lights and find Baker in bed with a single lamp. "Sorry I took so long. I couldn't figure out what I wanted to sleep in."

"Don't be sorry, come here," he opens the covers and then taps the bed to the spot right next to him. I jump in with him. He pulls the covers over me and then wraps his arms around me while I rest my head against his chest. "I can't thank you enough for everything and getting us an invitation to the gala."

"You got an invitation... so did I," he chuckles.

"It'll help us, so I'm thankful you thought of us" I snuggle up to him a little more, and he wraps his arms tighter around me.

"Will you be my date?" he asks me somberly.

"Of course, I'll be your date," I say, smiling against his chest

"Em, I can't think of anyone else I would want to be with that night," He says while brushing his hand across my back, giving me chills.

I'm speechless and don't understand how someone I despised for such a long time can treat me like I'm the most important person to him. Before I knew him, I would have never thought he could be the kind of person he has been with me. I want to think that this is how it'll always be with him, but then again, there was a time when I didn't hear from him for weeks. I don't want to fall into these gifts and his thoughtfulness until I know this is real, and until then, I will need to protect my heart because I am not ready for it to break again. So instead of answering him, I snuggle closer and enjoy this moment like it'll be like this forever.

Chapter Nine

Baker

Watching Emma's face light up last night when I showed her her surprise brings me so much happiness. There was a time when I never thought of doing these kinds of things for a woman until I met her, and I wanted to give her the world. I want to feel at home for her; she already means that much to me.

After taking Emma to work this morning, a new routine I enjoy, I walk into work. "Good morning, Mr. Hayes. You have a visitor in your office this morning waiting for you."

I don't recall scheduling any meetings this morning.

"Thanks, Marie. I'll let you know if I need anything today," I step up, wondering who could be waiting for me in my office.

When I open the door, I find my mother sitting in one of the chairs in my office. "Mom, what are you doing here? You didn't have to stop by. You could've called" she gets up from her seat, hugs me, and I kiss her cheek.

"I was in the area this morning; I thought I would stop by to see how you are doing. We haven't heard from you in a while" she retakes a seat.

I walk around my desk and take a seat. "Sorry, I've been sort of busy lately."

"Ryan says you have been seeing someone, is that why we

haven't heard from you? Who is she? Can we meet her?" she is grinning, excited.

I wasn't ready to tell my parents yet. I want to give Emma time to warm up to me before meeting my family. I know I want her to meet them, but she hasn't had her family in years, and I don't want to intimidate her. My parents have never met my girlfriends, so I know they are ready to see me with someone, but I know Emma wouldn't be ready for all the questions I know they would want to ask her.

"I have been seeing someone, but it's very new."

"Your sister will be in town Sunday, so that we will have our family dinner then. Will you bring her with you?"

"That seems too soon to be meeting my family, and I will have to ask her if she is comfortable. If she agrees, you will see the both of us on Sunday for dinner."

She smiles, "Well, hopefully, she would love to meet us. I think it's about time you find someone to settle down with, Baker. We want to see you happy."

My parents understand that work means a lot to me, and I haven't had the time to settle down with someone. They don't know about all the women I have been with. They haven't seen the pictures in the newspaper. I'm surprised she heard about Emma from Ryan; we have both been doing well with keeping our private lives to ourselves, besides talking about work. I would like to know Ryan's intentions behind that.

"I know, Mom, I know."

She gets up to leave, "I must get going. Before heading home, I have a few things to do in the city."

I meet her at the office door, hug her, and give her another kiss.

"I will see you on Sunday."

"Bye, my little Baker" she has always had that nickname for me. "Love you"

"Love you too, Mom," shutting the door after she walked out.

I will have to talk to Emma later about meeting my parents. I know she will win them over like she has me but is it too soon?

The day has been tedious, and I'm just ready to be finished with what meetings I have left scheduled so I can figure out some plans for Emma and me this weekend. The weather will be nice this weekend, so maybe I can take her to do something outdoors with me. Just when I'm thinking about her, my phone pings

Emma: Slow day here, what about you?

Me: Same. We're your ears burning, and I was thinking about you.

Emma: Thinking about me, Good or Bad?

Me: Good, of course. What are the plans tonight?

Emma: I need to go to my apartment after work for some things.

I frown, I'm not sure what things she needs to get, but it could be late when she's back home.

Baker: You want to watch a movie in bed when you get done?

The setup would be the perfect time to talk about Sunday with her.

Emma: Great. I'll see you later then.

It's just after eight, and I'm still waiting for Emma to come to the apartment. I assumed she would have been here by now. While sitting at the kitchen island, I picked up my phone to call her just as Ryan entered the elevator. "Baker, so good to see you today."

"If you had come into work today, you would've seen me. What are you here for?" now is not the time I want to talk with Ryan.

He makes his way to the living room, making himself comfortable on the sofa.

"Did mom come to see you today?" he knows very well she did.

"What are you up to, Ryan? Why did you tell her about Emma?" I get up and take a seat on the sofa opposite him.

"Just making sure you're still going through with our plan."

"You're being ludicrous."

Ryan should know that the agreement we had is off the table now. I told him about the night at the club and that I wasn't going through with it anymore. It was before things between Emma and I were serious. I'm seeing her because I want to, but he doesn't need to know my business.

"Now, why don't you get out here, and next time, let me know you're stopping by," I say as I get up from the couch to pick up my phone from the bar.

He gets up from the couch, pausing before he hits the elevator button, "I'll be seeing you on Sunday," he gives me a big grin and then gets in the elevator.

Once he's gone, I try to call Emma, and she doesn't answer. I hadn't heard from her since before she left work. She said she was walking to her apartment with Claire after work. She needed to grab a few things and then insisted she would catch a cab to get here tonight. I have this uneasy feeling that something happened. I knew I should've picked her up from work, helped get all she needed, and brought her home myself.

I again don't get an answer when I call her, so I send her a text asking if everything is all right. I wait for about ten minutes and nothing. I'm now concerned, so I grab my keys off the entryway table and rush to the elevator. I need to know where she is and if anything has happened to her.

I pull outside her apartment building, rushing up the stairs to get to her floor. Luckily, she gave me a key to her apartment. I unlock the door and rush in, yelling her name, "Emma" I look all around, opening the door to every room in her place, and she's not there. The place looks like someone hasn't been here in days. There is no sign of her stuff anywhere. I am now in full-blown panic mode. I rush out the door, thinking of the next place I will find her.

She could be at Claire's if she didn't stop by her place. I go down another floor and find Claire's apartment number. I have never been here, but I know her door from talking with Emma. I knock a few times, yelling "Claire," and I get nothing. I wipe my hands down my face and start pacing in front of her door. Maybe they are still at the flower shop if they aren't home.

I get into my car and speed off, calling Emma several more times with no answer. I leave her a voicemail, "Emma, please pick up. Where are you? I am worried about you."

I am trying to sprint through traffic, but all stoplights are backed up for days, with it being a Friday night. Bloom is within walking distance of Emma's apartment building, but it feels like it takes me hours to get there.

When I can finally see their shop in the distance, police surround it. My heart sinks, and I get this sick feeling inside my stomach. I do not even attempt sprinting through traffic anymore to get closer. I pull over, parking my car in the first open spot. I leave the car and take off, running towards the building.

There are police all over the outside and inside the building. I can see the front glass door is shattered all over the ground. I finally get to the front. I can barely contain my breathing, "What happened here? Where are Emma and Claire?" I try making my way inside when a police officer puts his hands on my chest to stop me. "Sir, you cannot go in there. We are going to need you to back up. We are investigating the scene."

"Investigate. Tell me what happened. Where are they?"

Are you family, sir? I can't give you any information unless you are family."

I'm so mad I can't see straight; I need to know what is happening here. I'm trying to catch my breath and thinking of a way to get them to tell me information.

"This is my fiancé's place; she owns this business. Can you please tell me where she is? I need to know if she's all right."

The police officer pulls me away farther from the front door. "Look, I can't be telling you this... there was a break-in. The women were inside when a robber entered the building. They're at the hospital around the corner. I think they will be okay from what I saw before they were taken away."

I instantly take off, yelling, "Thank you, thank you," while I run back to my car. Why are the girls at the hospital? I can't stop thinking about something terrible happening to Emma or Claire.

I pull up outside the hospital, parking by the emergency room entrance. I run up to the front counter when I make my way inside, "Can I help you, sir?" the lady behind the counter asks me.

"Yes, I need to see the girls that just came in for around the corner. Emma Adler and Claire Cassidy, can you tell me where they are?" I'm panicking and still trying to catch my breath.

"I'm sorry, sir but are you, family? I can't give you any information unless you can prove you are family," she says while looking down at her computer.

I'm pissed by now that I can't get any information about the accident or able to see either of them.

"Look...Emma, she's all I have. Can you please tell me where she is?" I say with my hands clasped together in front of me, begging her to give me some information. The lady at the front counter doesn't even answer when I spot Claire coming out of the double doors from the back rooms. She has a small bandage on her face and her arm in a sling.

I run over to her, "Claire, are you okay? Where's Emma? Is she alright?" she looks grateful to see me and gives me an unexpected hug. I embrace her tight, letting her know it will be okay. We let go of each other, and she leads me to some chairs in the waiting room.

"Emma is going to be alright," she looks at me with a sad look.

I feel a slight sense of relief come over me.

"What happened? Have you seen her yet?"

"They aren't allowing visitors for her just yet. They took her back for some scans. I was in the office when I heard a crash and then heard Emma scream. I ran to the front as fast as I could, but by the time I made it to the front, he had hit her over the head with a baseball bat that I think he used to smash the glass on the front door and started taking all the money from the register. I ran over to Emma, but she was knocked unconscious, so I tried to fight the guy away, but he threw me to the ground. I bumped my head and sprang my wrist when I fell. When I got back up, he had already left through the front, and I dialed 911 as fast as I could while trying to get Emma to wake up."

It's a problem, the worst feeling I've ever had in my life. Just knowing how scared they must have been made me sick. I could've prevented this from happening if I had just taken them home after work.

"Claire, do you guys have cameras in the shop so we can get whoever did this"

She gives me a frown, "No, we don't."

That will need to change, and I need to know they will be protected when they return to work.

"When did she wake up? Have you talked to her?" I'm trying to stay relaxed but anxious to see her.

"She opened her eyes just before the ambulance arrived, but she didn't say any words. The doctors have been keeping me updated on her since we got here. I'm the only person on her emergency list. How did you know where we were?" she looks up at the double doors while playing with the strap on her sling, and I know she is waiting for the doctor to come out with the latest update on Emma.

I lean over the front of the chair, resting my elbows on my knees with my head down, "I tried calling her several times, but when I never got an answer, I took off to check the apartments and then the shop after that. It was surrounded by police officers when I arrived, and I got one to tell me where I could find you two. I'm so sorry this happened, I should've come by after work, but Emma said she was going to her apartment for some things, so I just went home."

Claire puts her hand on my back and pats it, "Baker, this

isn't your fault. We didn't know something like this would happen."

We sit there in silence for another few minutes when a doctor comes through the doors, walking towards us; we both stand simultaneously.

"She's doing good. She is awake now. We took her back for some scans of her head. She took a pretty good hit, but the scans show no signs of trauma, just a severe concussion. She should be cleared in the morning to go home; we would like to keep an eye on her overnight. She may have severe headaches for a few days, but we will prescribe her some pain medicine and let her get lots of rest."

Whew, I feel like a mass amount of weight had been lifted off my shoulders, "Can we go back to see her now" I ask, looking at Claire.

"Yes, you can. She's in the room on the left down the hall."

"Thank you, Dr," I say as he makes his way back through the double doors.

I turn to Claire, "You go ahead. I can see her after you. I know you may want some time with her."

She giggles, "Baker, come on, we can go together."

I'm so glad she said that because I wasn't sure I could wait any longer to see her.

We both make our way down the hall when Claire says, "you can stay with her tonight if you want. Hospitals give me the Heebie-jeebies, so I don't think I'll want to stay."

"I'll stay; I can have Ryan pick you up to take you home."

"I'd like that, thank you," she smiles.

When we reach Emma's door, I let Claire walk in before me. I come around the corner of the door, and when I see her lying in bed with a small bandage on her forehead holding together a few stitches, my heart drops deep in my chest. I lean against the doorframe to stay back while Claire spends time with her.

"Emma, we have been so worried about you. We are so thankful you are all right," Claire says as she walks over, leaning over her and hugging her.

"I'm okay, guys. You don't need to worry. I don't remember what happened, but the doctors told me everything. How are you, Claire?" Emma says in a soft tone.

"I'm fine, just a little sprang wrist. I attempted to fight the guy, but he won and got away" she laughs, and Emma smiles. I don't know how Claire can be so fearless, trying to take a man down, but I'm thankful for everything she did and calling the police.

I take my phone from my back pocket to text Ryan to come to pick Claire up at the hospital, not giving him many details. I told him she could tell him everything.

Claire and Emma have a little more time together before telling Claire that Ryan is out front to get her. She gives Emma one last long hug and tells her goodbye. I follow her out to the hall, "Hey, don't worry about the shop. I'll have someone come out tomorrow to clean up the mess. Take a few days off while we get the shop back in order, and rest, sound good?" she's hesitant but then says "Okay. Take good care of my girl for me."

I grin. "I will. I'll be in touch to check on you too, Claire," she smiles and then walks down the hall.

I return to the room, and Emma is sporting a big smile when she sees me. I walk over, take her hand and kiss her on her palm. "You had me worried tonight."

"I'm sorry."

"Don't be sorry. I am the one who needs to be sorry. I should have stopped by after work to check on you and make sure you made it home. How are you feeling right now?"

She lays her head back on the pillow, "I'm just tired, I had a small headache, but they gave me something to take care of. I suppose I have a few stitches on my forehead."

"Just a few, but you still look beautiful," I smile at her. "I'm going to stay the night here with you, and they said you should be able to leave in the morning."

"Thank you, but you can go home for the night. There are enough people here to keep an eye on me."

"I'm not going anywhere, Em. I have been worried about you for hours, and now that I know you are okay, I'm not leaving" I pull up a chair from behind me, taking her hand before sitting down. "Now, you should probably get some rest."

"If you insist," she is already closing her eyes to get some sleep. I pull out my phone again to text Ryan to let me know when Claire is home. I told him to stay with her so he could keep an eye on her tonight. He texts back that she's good and he is staying with her for the night. We may disagree on most things, but Ryan always does what I tell him to do when I need him for something. I'm sure he doesn't mind when it comes to Claire.

I send a few emails to have some people discuss what we need to get the flower shop back together and get some security first thing in the morning. I can't change this ever happening to them again. I don't even want to think about what Emma went through tonight. It breaks me.

I check on her, and she seems to be resting well. I get up to turn off the tv in the room, dimming the lights so that it isn't completely dark in the room if she wakes. I sit in the lounge chair they have in the corner of the room, covering up with the blanket lying over the back. I won't get much sleep tonight, but I don't mind if I am here to be close to her.

Chapter Ten

Emma

I'd awaken to the aroma of one of my favorite things, "Good Morning," Baker says, handing me a fresh cup of coffee as soon as I open my eyes.

"Good morning"

He sets a big black overnight bag down in the lounge chair in the corner of the room, "I brought you some clothes from home. I didn't think you would want to shower here, so I didn't bring any toiletries. We're busting out of here after you get dressed. They already cleared you to leave"

"Well, thank you" I move to get up from the bed.

"How are you feeling this morning? You need any help." He comes over and helps us stand anyways.

"I feel okay, just sleepy" I stand up and go to grab the bag he sat down.

"Well, the bed is waiting for you when you get home. You can sleep all you want," Baker smiles.

His phone starts ringing, "I'm going to get this while you get dressed," and then he heads into the hall.

I make it to the bathroom well, shutting the door behind me. Unzipping the bag, I open it to find some Lulu lemon leggings, a sports bra, and a matching top. I'm not sure how long it will take me to get used to wearing all the new expensive clothes he got me, but you won't find me complaining about them. I dressed in everything he brought me and then threw my hair in a ponytail. I haven't looked in the mirror since the accident, and I'm horrified when I do. I run my fingers over the bandage covering the few stitches I have. I can't remember anything, but I know Baker must have been upset to see me looking this way. I zip the bag back and then put it over my shoulder. When I open the bathroom door, Baker walks back into the room.

"Are you ready?" he says as he takes the bag off my shoulder.

"Yep, more than ready," I say just as he grabs my hand, kissing my palm before holding my hand and walking us out of the room.

On our way home, we are in the car when it hits me that the shop is probably a mess that needs to be cleaned up. "Blooms…We need to stop by the shop. We were supposed to be open today. I'm sure it needs to be cleaned up. Can we stop by there?" I say while placing my hands on my chest.

"I already have everything taken care of. There are people there now putting on a new front door and cleaning it up, don't worry about it. You relax. You will have to be closed for a few days. Claire already knows that I have everything handled."

"You didn't have to do that, Baker."

He squeezed my hand quickly, "I didn't have to, but I wanted to. You two need to rest and worry about getting better. There is no need for you two to have to worry about the shop. It's in good hands, I promise."

We get out of the elevator, and I can smell breakfast

right when the doors open. I can't remember the last time I ate anything. I'm starving. I walk over to the kitchen island and take a seat.

"I knew you'd be hungry, so I had some food delivered."

"I'm starving," I make a plate, wasting no time eating.

"I have your prescriptions on the counter over there when you finish eating, that's if you need them," he sits down next to me

"I'm fine right now. Thank you. Did you sleep at all last night?" I ask.

"I slept enough. I arrived early to pack you a bag and grab a coffee because I knew you'd want it when you woke up."

I smile because he already knows me so well.

"I also set a big television up in the bedroom so you can watch anything you want while you rest," he makes a plate and joins me.

"Are you going to be watching anything with me?" I ask while taking a bite.

"If you want me to, I don't have any plans today" he turns to look at me.

"I'd like that."

He helps me up the stairs on our way to the bedroom when we finish eating. He already has the covers pulled down on my side for me to get in the bed. He has a couple of water and snacks on my side table. He had already thought about everything I would want and need while I rested.

"I'm going to shower," I tell him.

"Will you let me know if you need help or anything? I will

stay in here just in case," he sounds concerned.

"I will, but I think I'll be just fine."

I walk into the bathroom, cracking the door, not wanting to close it if I need him. As I turn on the shower, I hear the tv turn on in the bedroom.

I put my hand in to check the water temperature and removed my clothes. I take a glimpse of my body while standing in front of the mirror, I didn't notice any bruises earlier when getting dressed at the hospital, but I notice some large dark black and blue ones on my back when I turn around. I frown, turning my back to the mirror to get a better look. I'm not sure how I got them from the accident, but my guess would be from falling. I don't think he hit me with the bat anywhere except my head.

I open the door, get into the shower, and then shut the glass door behind me. I begin washing my hair, lathering it well since yesterday was hair washing day and it didn't get done. Once I finish rinsing my hair and washing my body all over, I stand under the shower, just taking in hot water down my back while I close my eyes. I try to remember what happened at the shop again, but I can't seem to picture anything but waking up at the hospital.

I turn off the shower, then get out to dry off. I wipe the mirror with a towel to take another look at myself. The shower helped bring some color back into my face, and I am starting to feel a little like myself. I drop the towel so I can lotion my legs and arms up, and then pull it back around me, tighten it up around my chest.

I head into my closet, still in amazement at all the clothes Baker gave me. I start feeling lightheaded, so I sit on the ottoman while deciding which comfortable clothes to wear. I'm sitting there for a second when I hear Baker behind me, "Hey, are you okay?"

I turn to look at him, "Just a little dizzy, I think."

He comes into the closet, "Here, let me pick something out for you, and I can help you get dressed."

I could use his help, "thanks."

He walks over to the section filled with t-shirts and drawers with nothing but leggings and joggers. "What were you thinking, sweats, joggers, leggings, or shorts?"

"Leggings are fine," I say, watching him go through the drawers.

He grabs a pair of black leggings and an oversized t-shirt off the hanger. It's like he already knew what I would've picked. He gets to the underwear drawer, "tell me which ones. I have no idea how to identify these" I laugh and then get up to grab just a basic black thong" I hold them up for him to see, "this is what you wear with leggings" he seems amused. "that's what you wear to work too because you left a pair here the night of our secret meeting" I laugh. After all, I remember not being able to find my underwear when I was trying to leave his place. I think about how far we have come from that night. I pull the black thong up my legs while still wearing the towel, then I take the leggings from him and pull them up until they fit comfortably. He's been watching me the whole time.

I turn around and drop the towel to put on a sports bra and the t-shirt without flashing him. I feel his hands touch my back, reminding me of the bruises I forgot were on my back. I feel his finger run across one of them, and then I turn my head to look at him. "I forgot those were back there... I noticed them before getting in the shower."

He has such a sad face, "Do they hurt."

"I don't think so" I pull my bra over my head, then turn around to look at him.

He puts his hand on my cheek, and the other rests on my hip. "I hate that this happened to you while I was at home. It's something I'm not sure I can get over." I look down, not wanting him to notice the tears in my eyes. "It's not your fault."

I slip my shirt over my head, and then we both head into the bathroom, where I brush my hair. He is silent while leaning against the bathroom counter, watching me while I finish getting ready.

"Do you want to lay with me? Can we take a nap together?" I ask him while we walk into the bedroom together.

"Sure, but I'm unsure how much sleeping I will do. I will keep an eye on you" I don't say anything else. I know he must be tired too. He heads into his closet, which is now in the bedroom since he gave me his. He takes off what he is wearing now, and I can't take my eyes off him while all he's wearing is a pair of boxer briefs.

He throws on a pair of shorts while I get under the covers in the bed, then he makes his way over to do the same. The tv was on while I was in the shower, and an episode of The Golden Girls started playing. I look over at him, "you watched this while I was in the shower"? He lays down, getting comfy under the covers. "I watched this with my mom when I was little; it was her favorite."

"I watch this all the time with Claire."

We are cuddled up for an entire episode when I realize he is sleeping. I knew he probably hadn't gotten any sleep the night before. I decide I should join him, so I get a little more comfortable and close my eyes to fall asleep.

When I wake up, I'm snuggling up to Baker's chest, my arm and leg wrapped over his body. I would guess that I took a nap for a couple of hours. I rub my eyes when he says, "About time you woke up."

I turn my head to look up at him, "How long was I asleep"? he looks over to the clock and then back at me. "Looks like you took a five-hour nap. I have been up for about an hour."

I lay my head back down on his chest, "I didn't think I was that tired."

"Do you want anything to eat? I could run downstairs and get snacks; we could watch a movie?"

I sit up and turn to him. "That sounds good."

He gets up from the bed, "Good because I have been hungry since I woke up. I have just been waiting for you" he grins while he leaves the room.

I pick up my phone on the side table to see if I have any missed notifications from Claire. I haven't heard from her since she left the hospital last night. I guess she is being watched by Ryan still.

It doesn't take Baker long to grab snacks and drinks from downstairs. I hear him before he gets through the doorway, "Here is what we have, popcorn, chips, Twix, and M&Ms. I also brought us two sodas" it was like he already had this stuff ready for a movie because I knew this isn't food he keeps in his house.

"Where did you get this stuff? I know you don't eat this."

He scowls at me, "I got all this before coming home from work yesterday. We said we would watch a movie in bed but didn't get to."

"Well, we are now," I say, trying to cheer him up. "What movie do you want to watch?"

He picks up the remote and goes to the movie section. "We can watch anything you want."

I think for a minute, "just pick a good rom-com, one you don't mind watching."

"How about this one?"

I look at the tv. Baker is on H*ow to lose a guy in 10 days.*

"Sure" I've seen it about a hundred times, but it never gets old.

He opens all the snacks, sets them between us so we can eat them together, and then hands me my soda.

"So, I was wondering why you needed to go you your apartment last night?" he says while picking up

I didn't know he was worried about why I needed to go there, "I just wanted to grab a few of my things to keep here, like girl stuff and some bathroom stuff I needed. You got me all these wonderful things here, and I just needed some of my things, you know."

"So, you just wanted more stuff you can have here so you can stay here most of the time?"

"Right, is that all right with you if I do?" I ask

He turns to me, resting his hand on my arm. "That's more than okay. That is what I want you to do. If I had it my way, you could get clear of your apartment and live with me, but I understand that it's soon, and you want to hold on to what you have in case something happens between us. I'm not saying something will, but I understand," he keeps blabbing like he is nervous.

"For now, I would like to keep my apartment. What this is between us scares me. I feel like it's sometimes this feels too good to be true. I want to enjoy what we have right now and savor these moments. I have never had anything like this with anyone else. I don't want to think this whole thing between us will crash and burn one day, but it could."

He lays back with his hand behind his head. I look over at him, he has something on his mind, but we sit there in silence for a few minutes. I didn't want him to be mad, but I needed him to know what I was thinking. He finally looks at me, "My mother came by my office yesterday morning."

He has talked about his parents a few times, but I know he doesn't see them often. "That is great. Why did she come to see you"?

" My sister will be in town, so they moved this month's family dinner to tomorrow night. She was wondering if I wanted to bring you. I talked to her this morning before we left the hospital and told her we wouldn't make it. I figured you wouldn't be up to going since the accident. I didn't want to leave you here while I went, and I wasn't sure if it was too soon for you to want to meet them."

"She knows about me...."

"Yes, Ryan had mentioned you to them. I couldn't tell them about you myself, but this morning I did talk to them more about who you are."

"Well, we should go if your mother expects us to come. I will be fine getting out of here for a few hours."

He gives me a cute grin. Maybe he didn't think I was ready to meet them.

"Are you sure you want to go?"

"Yes," I think it would be great to meet his family, but I know deep down that I am a little scared, considering I haven't been around family since before I lost my own. I think this is just what my heart needs right now, though.

"We can leave early if you'd like. It'll take us over two and a half hours to get there."

"Where exactly do your parents live?"

"The Hamptons," he says as if I should already know.

We pull up the driveway to Baker's parent's house, the most beautiful White beach house I have ever seen. The house is massive, but you can still see the ocean behind it. It makes me have feelings of home instantly. It reminds me of houses in Florida, where I am from, but they are much more expensive. The yard is covered with the greenest grass. The landscaping is full of lots of plants of many different colors. I could live in a place like this for the rest of my life and live my best life.

Baker parks the car, "Are you sure you are ready? We can turn around and go back home" he grabs my hand while I'm staring out at the front of the house.

I grin, "I'm ready."

Baker comes around to open my door and grabs the bag from my hand that we packed together this morning.

We don't even make it to the door before his parents come out from the front to greet us, "Hello, we are so glad you guys are here," his mother says. She is gorgeous and doesn't look a day over fifty. She is tiny, with medium-length dark hair and green eyes, just like Baker. She gives us both a hug, and she smells like just like my mother does.

"Well, you are just the cutest little thing," she says. I wore a long, baby blue, long, thin, strapped sundress with a pair of slip-on tan sandals, all picked by Baker, my hair down in wavy curls.

"Mom, Dad, I would like for you to meet Emma," he says while holding my hand.

"Emma, we are so elated to meet you!" his mom says with a huge smile.

"These are my parents, Jack and Catherine."

"It is so wonderful to meet you two," I smile.

Bakers' dad, Jack, hasn't said a word yet. He is just standing back and letting Catherine do all the talking. Jack doesn't look very old either, and he has lighter-colored hair like Ryan and looks like a serious person in business.

Catherine starts walking back to the house, "Come on inside, you two. Audrey and the kids are out back playing in the pool. Emma, we would love for you to meet them" we follow behind her.

Once we get inside, I'm greeted with the smell of flowers. Catherine has a fresh vase full of flowers in every room I can see, making me smile. The house is exactly how I pictured it decorated, Beachy blues and whites everywhere, and all white walls. I think of the room Baker had redone at his penthouse for us. He must have used the same interior decorator.

We make our way through the house and head out the double back doors to the enormous inground pool with a slide, and there is nothing but ocean views from all around. I see a woman lounging in a chair by the pool, and she must be Audrey, Baker's sister. She is Baker's twin, literally him in woman form. She is gorgeous and doesn't look like someone with two kids. She must work out like the rest of the family. I only hope I have a body like hers if I ever have kids.

She gets up and makes her way over to us. "Hello, I am Audrey, Baker's sister."

Before I can introduce myself, Baker says, "Sis, this is Emma," as he puts his hand on the small of my back. "Nice to meet you, Emma. Those two little ones in the pool are Cooper and Kate" I look over at her to see the two little kids playing in the pool. "Once they get out of the pool. I'm sure they will love to meet you."

"Emma, would you like something to drink or anything? We can have a seat out here and get to know you a little better. We would love to hear everything about you," Catherine asks, making her way back to the house.

"Water is fine, thank you," she heads inside the house, and Baker has me follow him to a covered outdoor dining table and chairs with a huge umbrella over it.

"You don't have to tell them all about yourself if you don't want to," he whispers in my ear after we sit next to each other. His whispers give me goosebumps, and he notices. He smiles at me before I say, "It's okay, I don't mind."

Catherine comes out carrying a tray with an expensive pitcher and glasses filled with ice. Jack is following her, and after Audrey says something to the kids playing in the pool, she joins us at the table.

"So, we are happy to have you here today, Emma. Tell us what you do for a living?" Catherine says as she fills all the glasses with water and hands them around the table.

"I own a Flower shop with my best friend, Claire. It's called Blooms," I say as I pick up my glasses, taking a small sip of water. Once I set the glass back down on the table, Baker takes my hand in his and places them on my lap.

"That is great, so you probably noticed all the arrangements in the house. I have bouquets delivered weekly from a local flower shop," she says as she sits back in her chair.

"I did notice. I will have to make some arrangements to bring back with you next time you are in the city" she smiles just as I finish my sentence.

"Oh, Emma, I would love that."

Jack interrupts, "So, how did you meet"? He keeps a serious look on his face, and I know he will be a hard one to please today.

I look over to Baker to answer because I'm not sure his dad would like to know we met at a bar, and we are not going to mention the "Secret Meeting." Baker clears his throat, and I know he will make something up. "I met her while I was out one night, her beauty entranced me that all it took was one conversation for me to want her, and we have been seeing each other since." He's only half lying, I guess. I interrupt, "I wish it were a more romantic way of meeting, but what can I say? He impressed me that night."

Catherine seems to be on to Baker. He must be a momma's boy if she can tell he is lying. "So, Emma, are you from New York City?" she asks.

"I am from Florida and moved here after I graduated from college. I dreamed of opening a flower shop in a big city when I was a little girl. So, once I got my business degree, my friend Claire and I moved here with what money we saved to open Blooms."

Catherine seems to please, "Emma, that is wonderful. It is not every day you meet someone who followed their dreams."

I blush, "Well, thank you. May I be excused; I need to use the bathroom" this is a perfect opportunity to take the attention off me for a minute, and they could ask Baker some questions.

"Yes, dear, the bathroom is the first door on the right down the hallway," she points in the direction of the hall.

"Thank you, I will be right back," I say, but I intend to take my time. I need a few minutes to myself.

I make my way down the hall, going into the loveliest bathroom I have ever seen, and then shutting the door, locking it. I didn't need to use the bathroom, so I looked around for a minute and then checked myself in the mirror. I look better today and did a great job covering my stitches with my hair. I wash my hands, take a few deep breaths, and then open the door to the bathroom. I am greeted by Baker when I walk out, "You alright?" he puts his hands on my shoulders, looking me into my eyes.

"I'm fine," I lie

"You didn't flush, so I take it you needed a minute," this threw me by surprise that he was spying on me.

"I just needed a minute, sorry" he wraps his arm around me in an embrace and whispers in my ear. "We can leave. I know this may be a lot for you right now."

I whisper, "I want to stay. I want to get to know them too."

He unwraps his arms from around me, grabs my hand, and leads me back to the backyard. When I got out there, I noticed Ryan showed up.

"Why hello, it's so good to see you here, Emma," Ryan says with a smirk. I can tell Baker isn't happy with him right now.

"Ryan," I nod.

"Well, I'm going to go get dinner started. You all have some fun out here," Catherine says as she walks inside.

Baker looks to me, "You want to get in? I want to play with the little ones for a bit."

"You go ahead. I'll hang out by the pool," Baker says before heading in to get changed.

I sit on one of the lounge chairs covered by an umbrella. The kids watch me as I take a seat, and little Cooper, who I would guess was four, swims to the pool and uses his hands to hold himself up on the side, "Who are you?"

"Hello, cutie, I am Emma; I came here with your uncle Baker. Who are you?" I get closer to him by sitting on the edge of the chair.

He looks at me like he doesn't want me here, wearing his little blue arm floaties, "I am Cooper, I am four years old. Are you going to marry my uncle Baker?" kids these days, but I am surprised I guessed his age right. "I don't know, Cooper, that is for your uncle Baker to decide."

He smiles at me, "Well, if he doesn't, I will. I think you are pretty."

I laugh, "Thank you, cooper, and you are very handsome. How about you play with your sister? I can talk to you more later, okay?"

"See you, Emma," he says as he swims off to play with his older sister Kate.

I relax on the chair, putting my sunglasses over my eyes and laying back. I could've put on a swimsuit to get some sun, but I wasn't about to do that in front of his parents. All the swimsuits Baker had for me in my closet were tiny pieces of fabric, and I'm sure he picked those out himself.

Thank goodness I put my sunglasses over my eyes because I watch Baker coming out of the doors in his swimsuit, and I about lose it. His abs are shining like he rubbed tanning all over them, and the V lines he has down there make me want to drop all my clothes and skinny dip with him. Baker rubs his hands through his hair while smiling at me, and he knows I'm checking him out. I smile back, and then he jumps in "Cannonball" and splashes water all over my legs. The kids laugh at him, and he swims over to them, saying, "Who's first?" Cooper doesn't want to wait. He yells, "me, me, pick me" Baker picks him up and then tosses him in the air. Cooper screams while laughing before he lands, splashing water all around him. Kate says, "my turn now" he picks her up and throws her, and then they all start splashing each other. I sit back and watch when Audrey comes over and sits in the seat next to me. "It's cute, huh? He always does this when we come here."

"It's super cute. I haven't seen Baker like this, so this is good," I say, keeping an eye on them playing in the pool. They have now moved on to Marco Polo.

"Sorry about my parents and their one hundred questions earlier. They did that with my husband when they first met him. He also left the table for the bathroom."

I turn to her, "Well, that is good to know I wasn't the only one. They seem great, and I know they haven't met any of Baker's girlfriends before, so I knew they would interrogate me a little."

"You like him, don't you," she asks while watching the kids playing in the pool with him.

I turn my eyes to them playing, too, "I do, but it's soon to tell where we will go. We have only been seeing each other a couple of weeks."

"I think he's falling for you. I see how he looks at you," I want to believe Audrey. I know he looks at me like I'm the only person in the room but is it real?

I don't even get to say anything to her when Catherine yells, "Would you two want to come help in the kitchen" Audrey and I look at each other; she rolls her eyes and then gets up off the chair, and I follow her.

Baker splashes me when I walk by the pool, giving me a wink when I look at him. My heart flutters

Catherine already has assignments when Audrey and I make it to the kitchen.

"Emma, do you care to make the salad? Audrey, you help cut some veggies."

"I don't mind, and I used to help my mom all the time in the kitchen" they both stopped to look at me. They already knew my parents had passed away and didn't expect me to mention them.

I give them both a look, “Baker told you, didn't he”?

Catherine goes back to what she was doing, “Oh yes, dear, we were told not to bring up your parents. We are so sorry.”

“Don't be sorry, and I brought it up.”

“Baker says you are quite the cook. He told us you made him lasagna that was to die for,” Catherine says while preparing some potatoes to roast.

“That Baker, I only cooked for him once. We just haven't had much time for me to do it again between work and the accident and all,” they both give me the same look they gave me just a second ago.

“Let me guess, he told you about that and not to bring it up. What all has Baker told you”?

“Honey, I think you did a great job already sharing the things we weren't supposed to talk about,” we all laugh.

We all get back to preparing the food for dinner. Jack comes in to grab the steaks for the grill. When I saw him, I realized Ryan must have taken off somewhere. I haven't seen him around in a while.

“So, Audrey, where do you live? Baker said you were in town to visit for the weekend.”

“We live in Chicago. My husband Clark owns a law firm there. He was busy with work this weekend, so the kids and I flew in to stay the week. Mom and Dad have so many extra rooms. You and Baker should stay here some time.”

“That would be nice. It is so much different out here than in the city. It would be a good escape for the weekend. This place reminds me of back home, and I like it here.”

Audrey and I finish up the salad, cutting veggies, when

Baker comes in with a towel around his waist, and the kids in towels follow him in. "We figured we better get out before we get wrinkles, or old man hands as Cooper likes to call it" he smiles, and Cooper laughs. Kate is older, so she doesn't say much around me.

Baker comes up behind me, putting his hand on my waist, and it startles me a little, "I'm going to go change. I'll be down in a minute," and then he takes off from the kitchen.

"Emma, do you want to help me set the table"? Catherine asks, with a stack of plates in her hands. "Sure" I grab the napkins from the top of the stack of plates and the silverware she had lying under them. We go to the dining room, where a large table seats twelve people. Catherine makes her way around the table, setting plates at each seat. I follow behind her setting down a napkin and then silverware on each plate.

> "You make my son happy, Emma" she doesn't look at me and continues setting the table.
>
> "Thank you, but how do you know? He makes me happy. He has done so much for me in the short amount of time we have seen each other"

"It's in how he looks at you that I know. He has told us all that he's done for you, and I'm not surprised; you are great for him. We are so happy you two decided to come today. I couldn't wait to meet you" Catherine sets down the last plate and turns to me with a big smile. She hugs me like she has done several times today. I can't help but think maybe she likes me, but maybe she also feels bad that I don't have any family. Once she hugs me, she says, "You don't have to call me Catherine; you can call me anything else you'd like"

While that is very sweet of her, I think for right now, and I will call her Catherine until I know in my heart that Baker is the one for me.

Chapter Eleven

Baker

We finish dinner with my parents, and I sit at the table with my dad while the women clean up the mess. Emma has done a great job fitting in with Mom and Audrey, but my dad is not coming around to her like I thought he would.

"What do you think of her dad"? I ask him seriously as I stretch my back in my chair and cross my arms.

He waits for a second, then looks around to see if anyone is around us. "Ryan told me how you two met. You don't have good intentions, Baker."

I shake my head. I'm pissed. "When I first met her that night, I was going along with Ryan's plan. Then I took her out, got to know her, and called it off with her and Ryan. I told him I wasn't going through with it anymore. She found her way back into my life, and I honestly can't see myself without her dad. She makes me want to be a better man."

"I'm not convinced on that just yet. Stop thinking you can do whatever you need to make more money. You are deceiving people."

I get up from the table, "No, Dad, you're wrong. That's Ryan. I don't even care if we get this deal anymore." I push into my chair and walk away from him to the kitchen.

I walk into the kitchen to all the women laughing while

washing the dishes. I see Emma drying off a plate and then setting it down on the counter. I walk up behind her, taking her hand in mind, "Care if I steal this one for a minute?" she turns to me, surprised.

"We don't mind at all," my mother says, still washing dishes.

"We'll be right back," I take her hand and walk out the back door.

"Where are you taking me?" she asks as we walk by the pool, making our way down to the ocean.

"Let's go for a walk."

The sun is starting to set, and it's the perfect time to walk by the ocean. I think for a minute that this might be the perfect time to tell Emma about the deal with Ryan. I know it'll upset her, but if she let me explain now, she won't get her feelings hurt if she ever finds out about it.

We are walking in the sand along the water, holding hands, when she says, "Thank you for bringing me here today. It means a lot to me to get to meet your family."

"You seem to have won everyone over, and it's like you belong in this family already."

I can see her give me a small smile, and I know something is on her mind. She is silent for a few minutes while we continue walking. I finally broke the silence, "What are you thinking about?"

"This place feels so much like home to me. Maybe it's around your family and then the beach. It just makes me miss my parents," we stop walking, and I pull her into my arms, holding her tight. I give her a small kiss on the forehead. Using my hand, I pull her chin up to look at she has a few tears rolling down her face.

“This is just a feeling I haven’t felt in a long time, and it’s a good feeling....”

I wipe away the few tears left on her face with my hand. We stand there for a little longer, watching the sunset. “We should come back here more often.”

“We should. I’m sure your parents wouldn’t mind us coming here now and then,” I know my mother would love that, but my dad, not so much. I need to prove to him that what Emma and I have is good.

I let go of her taking her hand in mine, “We should probably get on the road and head home. I need to go into the office tomorrow.”

“Can I stop by the shop tomorrow”? she asks me. I know she is ready to get back to work.

“It should be ready tomorrow afternoon. I can take you there when it’s done.”

We get to my parent’s house and say our goodbyes. Emma hugs everyone, and then we get on our way back home. It doesn’t take her very long to fall asleep. She did an incredibly fantastic job getting out today and getting to know my family after all that happened just days ago.

It’s Monday morning, and I’m getting ready in the bathroom, trying to be gentle, so I don’t wake Emma up. I wish I didn’t have to work today, but I have some meetings scheduled that I can’t reschedule. I got an update last night on the flower shop, and it’s already finished, so I will take her there tonight so she can see the changes I have made. I also have a few people scheduled for interviews so they can hire some help, they can cut back on their hours, and take off on Saturdays. I hope Emma doesn’t mind me just taking over.

When I come out of the bathroom, I notice Emma isn't in bed sleeping anymore. I leave the room to find her in the kitchen, pouring herself a cup of coffee. I go down the stairs, "Good Morning, rest well?"

She looks incredible wearing a silk pajama set, her hair up high in a messy bun, "I did, thank you. Want me to make you some coffee to go?"

"Sure. What are your plans around here today until I get back?" I go to the fridge to grab water.

"I think I will just hang around, probably do an order for the shop, and check in on Claire since I haven't heard from her in a few days." She says while making my coffee, then hands it to me.

"I should be back after lunch. With you being here, I don't want to be gone all day" I grab my work bag and then head for the elevator.

"Have a good day, Baker," she says from across the room.

"You don't have too much fun without me," I say, then get into the elevator.

I'm in my office finishing up some emails when Ryan calls me, "Where are you, Ryan?" I haven't seen you here today."

"I'm dealing with something right now. I will be back tomorrow, and I just wanted to let you know that," Ryan says in not his normal jerk tone.

"Is this problem the same reason you left early yesterday"?

"Look, I don't want to talk about it right now. I'll see you tomorrow," before hanging up. I didn't even get to ask Ryan about my conversation with Dad.

I don't know what's gotten into him lately, but he needs to cut his immature bullshit out. I don't think I can take much more of his games.

I hear a knock on the door before I can get back to working on emails, "Come in."

My assistant Marie opens the door, "Sir, you have a visitor," and then walks in Emma, dressed in pair of jean shorts, a dark green tank top, strappy sandals, and her long hair down with curls. "Hey, just thought I'd bring you lunch, you know to return the favor of you bringing me lunch. It may be the only time I get a chance to," I nod to Marie, and then she leaves, shutting the door behind her.

"Em, you didn't have to do that. How did you get here"?

"Don't worry, and I didn't walk. I took a cab and grabbed lunch a couple of doors down. I was getting lonely at home alone, and Claire hasn't been answering my calls," she sets the bag of food down on my desk.

She's taking the food out of the bag, placing my food in front of me. She got me a sandwich and then herself a salad. She starts eating when I tell her, "I'm glad you are here. I want to talk to you about something."

She frowns like I am fixing to give her the bad news, "I set up some interviews with a few people to work at the flower shop. It would be good for you and Claire to have a couple of extra hands so you two can get a break."

She's thinking for a second, and maybe she is mad at me.

"I think that's a great idea. Claire and I were talking about it before the accident. The business has been going well lately, and we have trouble keeping up with the two of us. I'm just worried about where we will come up with the money to pay them. Maybe hire one person for now and then figure out later if we can add a second person," she continues eating.

"How about you hire two, and I can figure out where the money will come from to pay them both. It would help if you didn't worry about it. You and Claire can start working shorter hours and taking off on Saturdays," She glares at me.

I take a bite, and before she can say anything else, I interrupt her trying to change the subject so she can't object to what I want. "What's with Claire? Why do you think she isn't answering your calls"?

"Maybe she's just taking a nap since we have the day off. I would think she would miss or check in on me, but I haven't heard from her since Saturday."

"You want to head over to the shop when we finish here, you can try to reach her again before we get there, and she can meet us."

"Sounds good," she says as she finishes up her salad.

After giving her a tour of my office, we headed to the shop. It would be the first time I would see it in person, too. I had some contractors send me pictures while we were at my parents to make sure it was what I had envisioned.

She gasps right when we pull up, "a pink door" she turns to look at me and then gets out of the car as soon as it stops. The once-glass front door that broke is replaced with a paneled modern glass and wood front door that I had painted a blush pink. I also had the front glass on both sides of the door replaced with something more durable, and they now have displays in the windows so you can't see straight into the shop.

She's smiling and giggling while I try to unlock the front

door. I open the door, and she heads in first. The once-colorful shop has been painted all white, with a huge brass chandelier hanging down from the center of the ceiling. The small wood counter is now a sizeable light wood counter with a white porcelain countertop. There is a small blush pink cushioned couch at the front of the shop and all-new work arenas that match the front counter at the entrance. I replaced all the coolers with stainless steel ones.

Her eyes light up, “How did you do all this in two days”?

“I might know a few people. What do you think”?

“I love it... I expected you to replace the door, maybe the front counter” she waves her hand around, “But all this... It’s Beautiful.”

“I had security cameras installed. You can check them from the office. There is one set at the front door and then two here.” I stand back with my hands in my pocket while she roams the place, checking everything out.

“I don’t know how I’ll be able to afford this. I know insurance paid for some, but I'm sure you went beyond what they gave us.”

“That’s the thing I need to tell you... I bought it,” Emma turns around, giving me a frown.

“Don’t be upset, but to do all this, I needed to own it, so I offered the guy you rent the place from a price he couldn’t refuse. So, I paid cash, and you owe me nothing.”

“Baker, this is great, and I love it, but this was my dream, not yours. I can’t just let you save me every time I need saving because you have money....”

I interrupt her before she says something she may regret or hurt me. “Em, I know this, and I know you work hard for everything you have... You are my dream, and I want to be the one to save you when you need saving. I know that you could care less how much money I have but just let me buy you the world if I want to because... I want to," she's still giving me a sad face, so I take her face into my hands, giving her a soft kiss. I have wanted to give her a kiss since the club night. I want her to know I'm serious about us, and I do want to give her the world.

She's taken back by me kissing her. She drops her head, looking down at the ground for a second, then says, "Can I work tomorrow, boss?"

I roll my eyes and then laugh.

Chapter Twelve

Emma

It's now Thursday, we have had the new shop open for two days, and we also have had tons of new business. I'm not sure if it was the new look or the fact that we were in the paper for being robbed. It doesn't matter which one because this new money flow has been nice. Now that we don't have to pay rent, we should start seeing more money in our bank accounts. We did hire two new people, Baker picked them himself since he is a boss man now, plus he had to make sure they were legit good workers and not criminals. He picked two sweet younger girls, Lexi and Liv, who were also best friends.

I didn't talk to Claire until she came into work on Tuesday; she said her reasoning for not getting back to me was that she was sick. She has been fine since returning to work, so I'm not sure if she was lying, but I can't ever be angry at her, so I'll go with it.

Claire and I each picked a new girl to teach the basics of bouquets. I have made Lexi into a pro; she makes some impressive arrangements. Claire is slacking a bit on Liv, so today, I plan to steal her away for a few hours to get her up to Lexi's speed.

I'm at the front counter checking on orders and watching Lexi make some arrangements by herself when I hear the front door open. I say, "Hello, Welcome to Blooms," while keeping my eyes on the computer.

"Emma," I know that voice. I look around the side of the computer, "Catherine, what are you doing here"?

She comes over to give me a hug, "Oh dear, I needed to see the new shop and order some bouquets to take back with me to the house."

"Oh yes, want me to surprise you with the arrangements, or did you have something in mind"? I ask her while I walk back to the front counter, and she joins me.

"You can surprise me. I trust you...Baker did a great job with this place," she says while looking around.

"The man has great taste," I say, giving her a grin.

"He sure does. He picked you," Catherine says, and I blush.

"So, I can work on those, you can wait here on the gorgeous couch, or you can swing back by in about an hour or so," I ask her.

"I'm going to visit the boys at their office. I will come back by before I head back home," she comes around to give me another hug before walking towards the door.

"Sounds great. I'll see you soon," I say as Catherine walks out the door.

When the door closes, Claire comes out from the back. "Who was that?" She walks over to me, still standing at the front counter.

"That was Baker and Ryan's mother. She just ordered some arrangements. I'm going to have Liv help me work on them."

"Their mother was here, ordering flowers,"? she says, like she didn't hear me right.

"Yes, she's a lovely lady. I met her on Sunday at their house in the Hamptons. She likes to keep fresh flower arrangements around the house. Did you get that?" I ask her.

"Heard. I'll be in the back office if you need me." She says as she makes her way to the back for the hundredth time today. I'm not sure what she is doing back there, but she has been slacking since the new girls got hired, and I don't think I can take much more of it.

"Hey Liv, you want to help with some arrangements"? I ask as I head over to my worktable, grabbing flowers with different shades of white, blue, and greenery that I think would be perfect for their beach house.

"Of course, I would love to," she comes over, grabs some vases that would pair with the flowers perfectly, and we get to work.

When we finish them, I find a couple of boxes to set them in, so they won't tip over when she is on the drive home. It only took us a little over an hour to finish them. We don't close for a couple more hours, so I will put an order in for flowers while I wait for her to return. The new girls have been working on orders, and last I checked, Claire was asleep on the desk in the back office. I thought about telling her to go home, but I didn't want to bother her.

I'm finishing up our flower order when I hear the door open, and I see Catherine and Baker walk in. "Hey."

"Did you finish, or am I too early?" Catherine asks.

"I finished them," I pick up the boxes and set them on the front counter. Catherine peeks inside one of them, "Emma, these are gorgeous. I have never seen anything like this before. You have quite the talent," I notice Baker smiles when she compliments me.

I blush, "Oh Catherine, you are way too kind... thank you."

"I'll take these to your car for your mother," Baker says, picking up one of the boxes off the counter. While he walks them out for her, Catherine walks around the counter to hug me, "I don't have time today, but next time we should do lunch."

"Yes, I'd love that," hugging her in return.

Baker comes through the door to grab the second box and goes back out the door.

"Thank you so much for the arrangements. I can't wait to set them out when I get to the house" she is headed towards the front door just as Baker makes his way back in the door.

"It's no problem, Catherine. Anytime you need more, just come back. We can do lunch next time. Be safe driving back home" I give her a grin while waving to her. Baker hugs her and tells her he'll talk to her soon, and then she heads out the door.

Baker is walking towards me. "You'll have lunch with my mother?"

I give him a smirk, "Of course, I would love to have lunch with her sometime. Maybe she can tell me some embarrassing stories about you" I point my finger into his chest.

He laughs, "There are no embarrassing stories. I was a good kid. If I had any, my mother would not be the person to tell you those. That would be Ryan or Audrey."

"Well then, maybe I can meet Audrey for lunch next time she comes to town" he smirks and then folds his arms across his chest while leaning against the counter.

"Where's Claire at today? I was hoping I could steal you from this place early. We can go on a date,"

I gasp, "What's a date? Come again? I haven't been on one of those in forever," He rolls his eyes at me, "Claire is in the back room. She has been in there all-day napping. I didn't want to bother her, so I let her be. She said she was sick over the weekend," Just as I say, she comes out from the back with a handprint on her face like she just woke from sleeping on her hand.

"I'm fine. Emma can leave. I can close this place up with the help of the girls."

I grab my purse from under the front counter, "Are you sure you are good for me to leave early, Claire?"

She waves her hand, shooing me out, "I'm okay, now get out of here."

Baker makes his way to the door, and I follow him, "Text me if you need anything. Bye girls, thank you for all the help today" Lexi and Liv wave at me while I walk out the door.

When outside, Baker's driver greets us, standing by the car with the door open for us. When I get to the car, I slide into the back seat first, and then Baker behind me, his driver shutting the door behind us. "Baker, shouldn't we go home to change? I don't feel dressed to go anywhere fancy,"

I wore one of the shirts he had made for the shop, a pair of jeans, tennis shoes, and my hair in a ponytail, my everyday work wear. "We are not going anywhere fancy. This date is something different, just for you," he takes my hand in his and then squeezes my hand.

I stare out the side window, trying to figure out where we are going while our hands settle in his lap. He does a great job surprising me with these things, and as much as I love them, I hope this one doesn't have anything to do with buying me anything. I love all the gifts and surprises, but I want him to know that I can enjoy the simple things in life more.

"How was work today?" Baker asks, breaking the silence. I didn't notice.

"It was great, busy. Claire hasn't been doing her best, so I had Liv help me with those arrangements for your mother so she could get in some practice. The new girls have been doing well. How was work for you today"? I keep my eyes on him.

"It was a long, I didn't have much on my schedule, so the day felt like it went on forever, and I was just ready to see you," we gave each other a sweet look, and he started rubbing my hand with his thumb.

The car comes to a stop. I look out the window and notice we park at the park entrance, which is not far from my apartment. His driver, Carlos opens the door, Baker gets out first, and I get out behind him. Carlos grabs a basket, and blanket out of the trunk of the car, handing them to Baker, "Here you go, sir, just message me when you are ready" Baker nods, then takes my hand as we walk through the entrance of the park.

"What are we doing here?" He stays quiet for a second, just walking through the park and holding my hand.

"We are going to have a picnic here. We have both been busy with work, the accident, and meeting my parents. I thought you might like to have an easy night out for once."

We make our way to an area of the park where there is no one around. He sets the basket down and then unrolls the blanket. "Here, let me help you set that out" I take two ends, and we work together, getting the blanket down flat on the ground. He picks up the basket, setting it on the blanket.

I get down on my knees on the blanket, and him joining me while he opens the basket. He starts by pulling out a bottle of wine, with two silver stemless wine glasses and then a box that you would think was cupcakes, but when he opens it, it's one of those fancy charcuterie boards but in a cute brown box. It's the perfect setup for a night like tonight. "Thank you for this. I think this is something I needed."

"Anything for you, Em, I know how much you like to walk through the park, so I thought, why not have a simple date night at the park."

He pours wine into one of the glasses, handing it to me, and then pouring himself a glass. "It was good meeting your parents over the weekend. I was surprised to see your mom come by the shop today. I didn't think she would want me to make her some arrangements."

He takes a drink, "Well, she likes you. When she came into the office today to visit, all she could talk about was you and how much she enjoyed you. You won her over, over the weekend."

I blush, "She's sweet. You are lucky to have such a great mom."

He grabs my hand, "Do you think your parents would have liked me?"

"I think so. My mom would have loved you and the fact that you spoiled me. My dad would've probably had a million questions to ask you to ensure you had the right intentions with me. I was always his little girl, and he was protective over me. He didn't like the idea of me moving a thousand miles away from him so that he couldn't watch over me. He would be proud of me for being with someone like you. I would say you do an impressive job taking care of me" I get comfy, laying out and propping myself up on my elbows.

He knows how sensitive the subject is for me to talk about them, so he moves on to something else, "Have you ever been in love?" I was not expecting that question. "I think I was once. I dated this guy for over a year during my junior year of college, and while things were good between us, he didn't support my dream of coming here one day, so after a while of knowing we wouldn't make it, I broke up with him. Have you ever been in love?"

Baker gets comfy on the blanket, matching my sitting position, "I can't say I ever have been. I spent a lot of years thinking I couldn't love someone. I was so focused on school and then opening this real estate office with Ryan that I never thought about being with someone I could be with forever."

His answer doesn't surprise me. He doesn't come across as someone who has been in love. I want to think he could be in love now, but I know it's a matter of him opening his heart up to fall in love. Same with me, though. My heart's broken and has been for years over the loss of my parents, and it will take more than gifts to make me fall in love.

"I'm glad we have that in common, the fact we both had these dreams that we wanted to accomplish. I had many people in my life that couldn't understand or didn't believe in me," I picked up some grapes from the box, putting one in my mouth.

"You should be very proud of yourself. It's not every day you meet someone who has a goal in life from when they were such a young age and fulfills them. I also think we have more in common than living our dreams." He says while grabbing something to snack on from the box.

"Really, what exactly would you say we have in common"? The sun is setting, and the string light is now lighting up the park hung throughout the area.

"Let me think about it… We both like food, pretty much any type of food. We both like wine" Baker holds his glass up, and I smile, "we get along well because we can agree on the same things."

He isn't wrong, but we have a few other things in common. When we are together, it is very effortless because we work well with each other; I know it's a good thing, but I feel like our days of being effortless with each other could come to a halt soon.

"We agree on the same things, but would you say we want the same things in life? I have been happy with my life, running my business, and such. I have become such an independent person since the loss of my parents, and while it has been nice being around you and you helping me when I need it, I'm just not sure exactly what I want right this minute."

He needs to know how I truly feel. It scares me sometimes to be with him. I can't just give him a part of my heart yet. That's if he even wants it.

Baker is giving me his serious thinking face, he's quiet for a moment, and I know he's trying to give me his best answer, "I'll be honest, the night I met you, I wasn't looking for anything. I'm not sure what I want right now either, but what's happening between us has been great, and I'm enjoying you, but I don't want us to push anything right now. Let's go with the flow we have been going to see what's next for us. I don't want to force anything, but I want you to know that I care about you."

"Well, thank you," I look at the sky full of stars, and he lays down next to me, taking my hand in his.

"Em, I do have a question for you, though. I know we just said we aren't sure what we want right now, and we both agree we should see how this goes for us, but there is one thing I am sure of, I want us to be official, and I want you to be my girlfriend."

"You want me to be your girlfriend"? I look over at him. This moment is unexpected from Baker Hayes; he doesn't make things official with any woman and wants to be with me.

He turns over, looking at me while placing his hand on my cheek. "Will you? I know it already feels like you are since we live together, but I want it to be official. This doesn't mean anything that we have already been doing will change. As I said, I don't want to force anything."

"Yes... I will officially be your girlfriend" he places a kiss on my lips.

Chapter Thirteen

Baker

It's been two days since Emma and I made things official, and I don't think I have ever been this content. She is turning me into someone I thought I could never be, and I want to be the most incredible man I can be for her. I want to say I'm not falling in love with her at such a fast pace, but that would be a lie. Laying with her under the sky full of stars in the park the other night was just the right moment to ask her what I had been waiting to ask her from the moment she gave me a second chance.

I'm waiting for the espresso machine. Then I will wake Emma up for her first Saturday off since opening her shop. I woke up early this morning and just laid there for over an hour watching her sleep with her messy bun and silk gown, laying over my chest, looking so perfect while she slept. I slipped out of bed without waking her so I could go downstairs to make her other favorite thing besides me to wake up to, coffee.

Emma has made plans today to meet up with Claire to get a dress for the charity event, and while I would rather spend my day with her, I decided to meet with Ryan to go golfing. We used to go together at least once a week but haven't been able to since last summer. I want to figure out what has been bothering him. Lately, he has been acting differently. I want to think he has also forgotten about Dave Riley's deal and won't be bringing it up today.

Once I finish in the kitchen, I make my way up the stairs. Placing her coffee on my nightstand close to where she is sleeping on my side of the bed, I brush my fingers across Emma's face. "Good Morning, babe."

She opens her eyes and then stretches her arms out, "Morning" I kiss her forehead before she sits in the bed.

"I'm going to jump in the shower to get ready to meet Ryan at the golf course in an hour. When are you meeting Claire to go shopping"? I make my way into the bathroom, leaving the door open so she can hear me.

"She's working till noon at the shop, but I will leave before then to get a head start. Thank you for the coffee."

I pop my head out of the bathroom doorway before I get in the shower, "No problem. I'll be quick so that you can get ready," she nods while taking a sip.

When I finish showering and getting dressed in my best golf clothes, I sit on the side bed while she finishes up her coffee and scrolling through her phone. "You want to hang out tonight when we finish our plans for the day?"

She grins, "I can make us something for dinner if you want me to."

"I would like that. The kitchen should be stocked with groceries to cook whatever you want. I shouldn't be long today. I'll let you know when I finish and am on my way back here," I kiss her before getting up for bed.

"Sounds good, have fun with Ryan today," she gets up from the bed, making her way to the bathroom.

"The keys to the Range Rover are on the entryway table for you to drive it today. Have fun," I smile and then leave. I catch a glimpse of her expression about driving her favorite car today.

I knew she would be excited if I let her have it for a day, maybe more.

I'm sitting in my golf cart, waiting for Ryan to show up. The golf course isn't crowded, so I signed us up today to play the full eighteen-hole. Hopefully, Ryan is up for the task.

I finally spot Ryan's car pulling in. He gets out and gets his bag out of the trunk. I drive the golf cart closer to him, "Hey."

"You ready to get your ass handed to you today"? He says, putting his clubs in the back of the cart.

I laugh when he gets into the cart beside me, "If anyone is getting their ass handed to them, that'd be you."

We pull up to hole one, and I tell him to go first. He gets his driver out of his bag and walks up to the spot he wants to tee it off. He puts the ball on the tee, then gives himself a few practice swings before he's ready to hit the ball. I yell out, "Good Luck" he rolls his eyes at me, annoyed, and then sets himself to tee off. He rips the driver back and hits the ball like he needs to blow off steam. I watch the ball go high and land right through some trees. I turn my eyes back to him as he's throwing his driver to the ground, and then when he's ready, he picks it up then heads towards the cart.

"Nice hit," I say.

"Your turn," he says with an eye roll.

I walk up to the same spot as him and put the tee into the ground, setting the ball on top of the tee. I don't even try out some practice swings. I get comfortable, swing my driver, and watch the ball land perfectly in the direction of the hole. When I turn to Ryan, he's already in the cart with his arms crossed over his chest, staring straight forward. I get in the cart to drive us down to our balls, "You'll get better. This is just the first hole," he doesn't answer me. I pull up to the trees. First, we both get out looking for his ball. I finally spot it sitting right between two trees, but there are trees all around us, so I'm not exactly sure how he will manage to get this ball out of there.

"Want me to help you get it..." he interrupts, "No, I got it."

I stand back so he can figure out a way out of this. When he grabs his club, then heads back to the ball, I walk back towards the cart, not wanting any part of getting hit. He gets a couple of practice swings and then gets set to hit the ball. He swings back with full force and then hits the ball. The ball bounces off one tree to another and then whacks Ryan right in the forehead knocking his hat off. He immediately yells, not in pain, yell. Not an I'm pissed yell. He picks his hat off the ground, puts it back on his head, and then throws his club straight into a tree, which comes right back at him.

I'm hysterically laughing right now. This is the best thing I have ever seen at the golf course. I can't stop laughing when Ryan walks by, "You are not to tell anyone about this."

I throw my hands up, "I didn't see anything."

We drive over to my ball, and I hit it straight to the hole. I'm not trying to brag, but I might be decent at golf. When I get back into the cart, Ryan seems to have cooled off just a little, grabbing a cold beer from the small cooler I brought.

"Why don't you tell me what's been bothering you lately? Maybe it'll help ease you up so you can play golf?"

"You know we don't share our private lives," he takes a sip of his beer.

"I know, but you can talk to me about whatever is on your mind. I've noticed you have been distracted lately,"

I park the cart to the side to hit my ball. He doesn't say anything, so I knock my ball in the hole so we can move on. I put the ball in and then put my ball in the putter in my bag. Ryan is on the driver's side now, so I slide in. "Don't get angry, but I have seen Claire more than you know. Emma doesn't know either, so don't get mad at her."

"And why do I feel like there's something else to this story? I don't see a problem with you dating Claire,".

He is silent for a second and then says, "That's all. There's nothing else to talk about. We don't want you or Emma getting angry that we have been secretly seeing each other. Claire doesn't know I am telling you this, so don't mention it to Emma until Claire has a chance to, okay."

I still don't trust him when he says that there isn't something else going on with him and Claire. He should know that we don't have a problem with them seeing each other. I know Emma will be disappointed that Claire has kept a secret from her.

Ryan and I finished the rest of the eighteen holes I signed us up for, which was a terrible idea given that it's been a while, and he had a lot of things on his mind. He didn't get much better at playing, but he didn't get worse. It was quite the show for today, and I'm sure he won't ever want to talk about this day again.

When I walk through the doors at home, the smell of pizza greets me. I love the smell, I thought I would be coming home to Emma in the kitchen cooking, but instead, she's lying across one of the couches with bags spread across the floor.

"I take it you found what you were looking for today," I smirk before joining her on the couch.

Her eyes meet mine when I take a seat. "Oh, I found a few extras and what I was looking for. My feet are killing me from all the shopping. We must have tried on hundreds of dresses today, then shoes and accessories. It was exhausting, but I'm all set for the event. Also, sorry about dinner. I picked us up some pizza instead."

"I'm also tired from eighteen holes of golf with Ryan. Today was not his best day, so it took us way longer than I imagined it to take us to play, so pizza is perfect for dinner," I stretched my arms across the back of the couch while she put her feet on my lap.

"Did Ryan mention anything about Claire?"

I can't lie to her. She doesn't need to know exactly what he said. "He mentioned he had been talking to her some, but that was about it, and I didn't want to invade him with questions, so I didn't ask him about it."

"Claire slipped his name a couple of times while talking today, but I don't think she caught that. I noticed it. You think they have something with each other that they haven't told us?" she gets up from the couch to head to the kitchen.

I know the answer, but I know Claire needs to be the one to mention it to Emma.

"You should ask Claire about it at work on Monday. Maybe she will tell you something."

She takes some plates out of the cabinet and then points to the pizza boxes. "You want any of this? I'm starving."

I get up to meet her in the kitchen, "You're always starving."

She takes a huge bite of her slice of cheese pizza, leaning against the kitchen island. She shrugs her shoulder, saying, "Well, I like to eat."

She is standing there eating, which might be a turn-off for some, but I think she looks adorable in her blue dress sundress, sandals, and wavy hair. It's the perfect opportunity to ask her another question I know she'll appreciate. I walk over to her holding out my hands for her to take. When she takes them without questions, I pull her up, putting one of her hands on my shoulder, the other in mine, and my other hand on her waist.

"What are we doing"? she says, looking into my eyes.

"Want to practice our slow dance for next weekend?"

I glide her around the kitchen, slow dancing. She gets more comfortable and closer to me while going around. I catch a small smile on her face before she puts her head against my chest, wrapping her other hand around me.

We go about this for a few minutes when she says, "I know what you're doing, Baker Hayes." I got a smile on my face because that's what we're doing, but I didn't want to be the one to tell her. I wanted her to notice. I want her to know that I remembered what she told me about her parents, and I wanted to be the one to recreate it with her because I'm falling hard. I kiss her on the forehead, and this is a moment with her that I never want to forget.

Chapter Fourteen

Emma

We are a few days away from the charity event, and I have barely spoken to Claire this week about Ryan. While shopping for dresses, his name seemed to pop up a few times while talking. I know they have been in touch with each other. I'm just unsure what's going on between them, and why she seems so secretive about things lately.

"Hey Claire, can I talk to you in the office?" I ask after putting away an arrangement in the cooler.

Claire is standing at the front counter on the computer, "Yeah, sure."

We make our way to the back office, taking seats across from each other. I want to see if she has been hiding anything from me.

"So, what's up?" She asks me while looking nervous.

"I want to ask you if anything is going on that I need to know about. I feel like you have been different since the accident, and I didn't know if there was something you wanted to tell me."

She tilts her head to the side, looking at me, "Everything is good. I promise I haven't been hiding anything from you. I will let you know if there is something, okay."

"Okay, I trust you. I just wanted to check. So, we are

good?"

She hesitates, then says, "Yes, we're good."

We get up, and I hug her. "If anything is going on, I want you to know I am always here for you."

"I know, Emma, thank you."

We both leave the office, and while I would like to think she is telling the truth, I still feel like she is hiding something because she never acts this way.

We have been friends for too many years, and I know when something is bothering her. I wish I could figure out what and why she doesn't want to talk about it.

While finishing up some arrangements with the help of Liv and Lexi, I hear the front door open, and I'm surprised to find Catherine walking in. "Emma, I have missed you. How are you?"

"Catherine, it is so good to see you," I greet her with a hug. "What are you doing here today?"

"Dear, I was just in town for the day and was wondering if you would like to join me for lunch?"

"I would love to let me finish up this, and then we can go."

She goes to the blush couch at the front of the store to take a seat, "Take your time, honey. It's no rush."

I nod, then hurry up, finishing up the arrangement I started.

Once done, I grab my purse from the back, and we make our way out the front door.

"You want to walk down to the Sandwich Shop? It's an excellent place for lunch. "I ask her while pointing in its direction.

"Sounds good, dear."

We make our way down the sidewalk, "So, does Baker know you are in town for the day and going to lunch with me?"

She is wearing black slacks, a white silk tank top, oversized sunglasses, and black sandals. She looks lovely for a warm day like today. Maybe she is in town for something important.

"He doesn't know I am here today. I am in town to help with some of the decorating for the charity gala this weekend and thought I could meet you without letting Baker know first" I didn't know she also helped with the charity event.

"Will you be at the Gala this weekend too?"

"Yes, dear, the whole family will be there. Jack and I always make an appearance to donate our funds, and after just a couple of drinks, we always leave."

"Well, I look forward to seeing everyone there. It is my first time going, so I am excited to represent the flower shop."

We get the Sandwich shop. I open the door for us, letting her walk in first. We go to the front counter to order two chefs' salads with water, and then we find a table towards the back of the restaurant that is more private to have a seat.

"So, Emma, how have things been with my son?"

"Things couldn't be better. You did a wonderful job raising him. He is quite the gentleman. He is very attentive, making sure I am always happy."

"That is good to hear, Emma. I have never seen him like this, and I am not sure I want to see him again the way he was before you. He is delighted with you, Emma. I think you have transformed him for the better. So, thank you."

"That is very nice to hear, Catherine" I take a sip of my

water. I wonder if I should text Baker to let him know I am with his mother for lunch.

"We all like you, Emma. Do you think you and Baker will get married?"

I almost spit my water out. Marriage is not something I want to think about right now. While I do like Baker very much, I don't think it is something we are both ready for. We have only been together for such a short period.

"Oh, Catherine, we haven't talked about that. We haven't been together long. I like your son very much, but I also think I am not ready for marriage. My heart still needs more time."

"I understand. It is hard to think about that when your broken heart still needs to be mended together. I want you to know I lost my parents at a young age, just like you did. I met Jack shortly after losing my parents, and I regret all the time not opening my heart to him sooner so that I could have loved him longer. I waited until we were pregnant with Audrey, and I wish we had more time to love each other before we had kids. It strained us for years, holding back feelings with him and closing myself off. I don't want you to make the same mistake as me, and I want you and Baker to have the happiest life together. I want the best for him. He is my baby. Baker got his name from me, my maiden name."

"Well, Thank you. Your son does deserve the best, Catherine. I want him to be very fortunate, and if he chooses me, I will try my hardest to give him the best life." The waitress brought our food, setting it in front of us, and it interrupted what I was going to say. Before I could remember what it was, Catherine asked, "Do you want kids"?

I pour the dressing on my salad, "One day, but not anytime soon. I want to spend a few years together before we bring kids into the mix."

“That is good. I would love to have more grandchildren, but time together before kids are so important,” she takes a bite of her salad.

I know I should be dreading the questions she is dodging at me, but I’m not. I don’t want to hold anything back from her, and I feel very comfortable talking with her.

We spent the rest of our lunch talking about other things, and then when we finished our salads, we walked back down to the shop, where I made up one quick bouquet for her, wrapped it in brown paper, and then gave her a huge hug before she left.

I make it home before Baker does, so I shower before heading downstairs to the kitchen to make something quick for dinner. Once I finish showering, I put on some leggings with a matching sports bra while letting my hair dry and then turn on the tv for some noise since it's quiet.

I’m searching through the fridge to find something to cook when I hear the doors open. I turn to find Baker walking in a while, talking on the phone. He holds up one finger to tell me just a minute and then walks upstairs to the bedroom. I watch him walk up the stairs, enter the room, and then turn back to keep searching. I find a couple of steaks and ingredients for a salad. I pull a skillet from the cabinet and get the steaks going while I chop some vegetables for the salad. I look at the bedroom door again, thinking Baker should be coming out anytime now, but he’s still in there.

I finished tossing everything together in the salad bowl, and the steaks were almost finished when Baker came out of the bedroom. I watch him walk down the stairs, wearing only a pair of black gym shorts, hair wet like he just took a quick shower. I can’t take my eyes off his glistening abs and his shorts hanging so low it's almost like he's asking to take them off. When he makes it into the kitchen, he comes up behind me, placing a kiss on my cheek,

"How was lunch with my mother today?"

I'm plating our dinner, "It was wonderful. Was she the one who told you we had lunch?"

He grabs the plates after I finish putting everything on them and then sets them on the two barstools we sit at when we have dinner. "I saw her at the ballroom setting up for the charity event when I went there to check on things today. She said she just got back from lunch with you. I wasn't surprised you two had lunch. She has wanted to get to know you better."

He sits while I grab two glasses of water from the fridge, joining him. "She came by the shop and asked, so we walked down to the Sandwich shop. She did ask some tough questions, but I know she is just looking out for you."

I am cutting into my steak when he says, "You are still here, so I'm guessing she didn't say anything to frighten you off."

I laugh, "She did ask if I wanted kids, but other than that, everything was normal questions."

He takes a bite, and I can tell he's thinking about something. I didn't want to stay on the subject, so I asked him how his day was.

"It was busy. I finished up some things at the office to help with anything at the ballroom for the next few days. Are you ready for Saturday?"

"I am. I didn't know until today that your family would be there."

"We have a whole table just for our family. This year though, we added you and Claire to the table with us."

"Well, thank you, but you didn't have to do that."

"Em, you are my date. I want you to sit with us, and Ryan insisted that Claire sit by him," he throws his hand up.

I'm not going to ask why they needed to sit by each other. Claire told me today there wasn't anything she needed to tell me, so maybe Ryan is just being friendly.

We both eat the rest of our dinner. Baker's phone rings while I take our plates to the sink. "I'll be back. I need to get this,"

I nod, and he makes his way back to the bedroom. I load the dishwasher and then clean up the rest of the kitchen while he is on his call. When I'm done, I sit on the couch, propping my feet up on the coffee table. I flip through the channels to find something to watch on tv.

I have been waiting for him downstairs for over an hour, and I'm too tired to stay up any longer, so I go upstairs to bed. When I walk through the bedroom door, he is no longer talking on the phone but instead typing something on it while sitting on the side of the bed. I walk past him to use the bathroom, "I'm sorry, Em, I have been dealing with some stuff for the event on Saturday. We were supposed to have a delivery for all the table decorations yesterday, but somehow all the stuff is running late and won't arrive until after the event. So, I have been dealing with the event coordinator all night to get something else going for the tables, and she just quit on us."

I stop at the bathroom doorway, "Claire and I can make some arrangements for centerpieces. We have enough flowers in stock to come up with something simple."

"Are you sure? My mother mentioned that idea, but I told her you would be too busy. We can figure something else out so you can spend the day getting ready."

"No, Baker. I would love to do that. I can get started on

them tomorrow and have them all done before Saturday, so I won't have to do anything but have them delivered. It won't be a problem at all, promise."

He gets up from the bed, wrapping his arms around me. "Babe, I should've asked you hours ago. Then I could've spent my night with you instead of worrying about all this."

I laugh, "It's alright, but I am going to bed now. We have all weekend to spend some time together."

We have been slammed at the shop today. We are working on all the arrangements for the ball, and we also have regular orders we have to do for the day. When I agreed to make the centerpieces for the ball, I didn't realize there would be fifty tables. We decided to make as many as we could today, and we will finish the rest tomorrow so that our delivery drivers can take them over to the ballroom on Saturday. Claire and I will then distribute them on all the tables.

The event theme is black and white, so we made simple arrangements with a mix of white roses, greenery, and just a few stems of eucalyptus. We had to put in an overnight delivery order for more white roses to be delivered in the morning, but we have enough for today. I have Lexi and Liv working on the incoming orders while I am at the same workstation as Claire, so we can ensure all the arrangements we put together to match each other.

"Baker said you are sitting with Ryan at our table on Saturday," I say, and Claire looks at me like she doesn't know.

"Really. Ryan didn't tell me that,"

"Are you two like a thing now?" she doesn't seem impressed with me asking her that.

"No! Why would you think that?"

"Well, you have been acting weird. Then he wanted you by him the table Saturday. So, I just figured you we were dating and didn't want to share yet."

"We are not dating. We talk sometimes," Claire says, giving me no eye contact, just keeping herself busy with the flower arrangements.

"If you two decide to date or anything, we don't have a problem with it. I think it would be fun, dating brothers, you know. Since we are sisters," I smile are her, but she gives me a half smile and doesn't respond, meaning she doesn't want to talk about it.

Chapter Fifteen

Baker

Saturday is finally here, the day of the Charity gala, and I'll finally share that I am a taken man. I can't wait to take Emma as my date; I am a lucky man.

Emma and I just arrived at the Windsor ballroom this morning, so we can put out the centerpieces she made for the tables, and I can finish up any of the last-minute things that need to finish before tonight.

I'm holding her hand as we walk through the doors into the ballroom, "Wow... Baker, this place looks fantastic. The arrangements will look perfect here."

The ballroom is ample, with light hardwood floors and high ceilings. The place is decorated with black tablecloths on all the round tables around the middle of the room. The chairs have white covers with a silk ribbon tied around the back to match the tablecloths. There is a massive stage at the front with a podium in the middle. It has tables behind it that will hold all the items for the auction. A dance floor is set up between the stage and all the dining tables.

"Thanks, Babe. It'll look better once we get everything set out."

She's checking her phone and then says, "The arrangements are here. The delivery driver is going to meet us out front."

We go out the front door, and I grab a cart for the arrangements before heading out. We open the delivery van's back door, filled with the most beautiful arrangements.

"Em, you did all these. They will look incredible on the tables."

She smiles and then starts helping me load them onto the cart. Once the cart is complete, we roll them into the building. She starts grabbing them and placing them on all the tables, and I follow behind her placing the rest on the other tables. When we finish placing all the arrangements, she helps me gather all the table setting supplies and the name cards for all the tables.

She starts with the plates and napkins, and I follow behind her with the silverware. After we get all that set up, we check the chart to find out where we need to place the name cards on specific tables. She is very organized, so we get everything done earlier than I imagined it would take us.

Once we finish with all the tables and the rest of the decorations, we get ready to leave. The ballroom looks phenomenal, and I think it looks the best for this event, all thanks to her help. I may have to hire her for next year's event, and we make a great team.

We get home after leaving the ballroom, and the living room is set up with a station for Emma to get ready. I hired a makeup artist and hairdresser to help her get ready. "Baker, you shouldn't have!" she's shocked

"Well, it's the least I could do for you since you helped me with the event"

She gives me a quick hug and kiss, then takes a seat to get ready.

"I'll be upstairs finishing up some work from yesterday; if

you need anything, just let me know, okay."

She gives me a thumbs up, as she's getting special treatment.

I grab my laptop from the kitchen island before making my way up the stairs into the bedroom. I sit on the bed and answer a few emails I couldn't get done yesterday.

I get out of the shower and put on sweatpants from my closet. I haven't seen Emma yet, so I peek my head out of the bedroom doorway and see they are close to having her done with her hair and makeup. We have an hour before we leave, but I decide to get ready, so I can leave the bathroom for Emma to finish getting ready.

I wear my suit, black pants and a jacket with a white button-up shirt. I'm looking in the bathroom mirror, tying my black tie, when I hear Emma come in, "Oh, I like Fancy Baker. You look good."

Smiling at her, she looks gorgeous with her blonde hair in big wavy curls, one side pinned behind her ear and the other hanging over her shoulder, her makeup is more than I have ever seen her wear, but it looks great on her.

Once I finish with my tie, she heads into her closet, "I'll head downstairs so you can finish getting ready." I know she wants her dress to be a surprise, and as much as I want to stay up with her to get ready, I want to wait to see her.

I go down the stairs to call my parents to check on them. I sit on one of the barstools, "Hey, are you and dad almost to the Windsor?"

"Yes, dear, we should be there in about fifteen minutes. Are you two ready to go? How does Emma look?"

"She is still upstairs getting ready," I look up at the

bedroom door "she should be done soon, and then we will be on our way. They have the runway for pictures, so make sure you park in front of the Windsor."

"We sure will, honey. We can't wait to see you two there. Love you, son."

"Love you too, mom," then I hang up the phone.

I'm setting my phone down on the counter when I hear Emma say, "Ready?"

I see her coming down the stairs, wearing a long white silk dress that dips in the front. The straps are diamonds that come around both of her shoulders. The dress hangs low in the back, with a slit on her right leg that comes up to her thigh. She paired it with a pair of strappy heels that matched the straps on her dress. She looks breathtaking; I am so taken aback by this moment that it leaves me speechless.

She reaches the bottom step, and I take her hand, kissing her fingers. I spin her, "Well, what do you think?"

"I think I will be the luckiest man there. You look phenomenal."

She blushes, "Let's get going. I don't want to be late."

"You sure you don't want to go back upstairs? We can enjoy a night with just us. I'm afraid someone will try to steal you away from me tonight."

She laughs, "Come on, we don't have to stay long."

Carlos already has the car ready for us when we exit the elevator to the front of the building. Emma gets in, I slide in behind her in the back seat, and my driver closes the door behind us. I grab her hand, lacing our fingers together, resting them on my lap, and then give her hand a grip. "What did you donate? I forgot to ask you earlier today?"

She turns her head to look at me. "Claire and I decided to donate a year of bouquets. Whoever wins it will get a fresh bouquet twice a month. What did you donate?"

"I donated the building for the event, and then I made a cash donation. There's not much you can donate when you're in real estate."

She gets silent for a few minutes, and I brush my thumb across her knuckles to help ease her nerves. I know she is anxious.

We finally pull up out front, and I get out and then take Emma's hand to help her out of the car. I feel so good having her by my side for this event. Before we make our way across the red carpet, they have lined up out the door for pictures, and I see my parents over on the other side. I wave and point them out to her so she can see where they are. Emma waves and my mother has a big smile, which tells me she approves of us. I give her a grin and then watch my parents walk into the ballroom.

We make our way down the runway, stopping right in the middle, where they take pictures of entrances. I place my hand on the small of her back while she places one of her hands on my chest, smiling. We get a few pictures before I take my hand, pulling her chin up to me, placing a kiss right on her lips in front of everyone, a kiss that we haven't had before. It's a kiss of telling her I love her without saying it. After a moment, she pulls back, looking me right into my eyes, and gives me a sweet grin, and I take her by the hand again and lead us in the doors.

"What is the look you just gave me?" she asks.

"What do you think it was"

She doesn't even get to say anything when my mom comes right up to her giving her an embrace, "Emma, honey, you look stunning."

"Thank you, Catherine, you look amazing."

My mother is wearing an all-black halter long sequined dress. "Hello, Jack," he gives her a nod. My dad must still be hanging on to the stuff Ryan told him. I am going to need another conversation with him before long. "Emma, let's go get a drink before this gets started… We will see you at the table" I nod to my parents, then we make our way to the bar table. The line is lengthy, so it may take a few minutes to get our drinks.

"If you would like to go around to talk with some people, I'll wait for our drinks," I say before she looks around the room and then turns back to me.

"You know what to order me. Just come find me when you are ready," she waves her hand as she takes off in the direction of Claire, who happens to be with Ryan close to the dance floor. They are talking with some of the people over the event.

I look around the room while waiting in line to see if there is anyone here I know besides the people who come here every year. While looking around the room, I lose sight of Emma.

I order her a red wine and myself scotch on the rocks, and once I'm handed our drinks, I go in search of her. I spot Claire, so I walk towards her taking a sip of my drink when I am on my way.

"Claire, have you seen Emma around here" Claire is dressed in a long black strapless dress, long red hair down with curls and black heels. She points in the direction of the dance floor.

"I saw her talking to a man over that way just a second ago," I turn my eyes and spot Emma talking to Dave Riley, his hand on her back. I'm immediately tense up, I have no idea why he is talking to her or how he knows her, but I will not let him put his hand on her. I take quick steps to get over to them as fast as I can without running.

I'm walking up on Emma from behind so she doesn't see me, and Dave Riley takes his hand off her once he spots me coming their way. I wrap my arms around Emma's waist, taking her by surprise. "Hey, Dave. I see you met my girlfriend. This is Emma Adler."

"Well, Hello, Mr. Hayes. I didn't know this gorgeous woman belonged to you. Emma, I know we have met before, but I am Dave Riley. I do business with Mr. Hayes here."

I am shocked by what he says, "You two have met before?"

"Baker, remember when I told you the boy knocked me over in the park? Dave was the one who helped me up," it comes to me whenever she asks me if I remember. That was the night she cooked for me at her apartment.

"I do remember. Thank you for helping her that day," I shake hands with Dave.

"It was no problem. It's not every day you can save a pretty girl from falling," he grins, and I want to slap it off his face. I sense that he knew who she was, and the accident wasn't an accident.

"It was good seeing you here, Dave. Em, would you like to go to our seats? This should be starting soon" I grab her hand.

She holds her hand out to shake Dave's hand, "It was good to see you again, Dave, have a great night" then we walk away.

We get a few feet away from Dave, "What kind of business do you have with him?" this isn't where I should tell her how we know each other.

"We can talk about it another time...."

We get to our table, and everyone is already sitting in their seats. I pull out Emma's chair for her, and she takes a seat seated by Claire. I take my seat, which is between her and my mother. "Hello, everyone," my mother is always the conversation starter.

"Catherine, what did you donate for tonight"? Emma asks.

"We always donate a three-night stay for our guest house in the Hamptons."

"Oh, that sounds nice" she gives me a stare that tells me she wants us to win it.

"So, Claire, I was wondering what has been going on between you and Ryan."

Surprised by the question, Claire looks down while playing with the tablecloth, "Ryan and I have become friends. Since Baker and Emma started dating, we have been spending more time with each other, but we are nothing more than friends," I am so confused by her answer, considering Ryan told me they have been seeing each other. I guess they decided they were better acquaintances.

"How long have you and Emma been friends?" Mother with her questions.
Claire and Emma look at each other, and then Claire says, "We have been friends since we were eight, almost two decades, so we are essentially sisters."

Before my mother can ask any more questions, the city's mayor takes the podium on the stage, and we all turn our eyes to him, "Good Evening, everyone. We are so happy to have you all here. We look forward to this event to raise money for different charities every year. This year we have decided the donations will go to Children's hospitals." Everyone starts clapping.

"Before we get started this evening, we would like to thank a few businesses that helped put this together tonight. First, thank you to Baker and Ryan Hayes for letting us have the event in this beautiful building" Emma turns, smiling at me, then rests her hand on my lap. "Also, thank you to Blooms flower shop for the most amazing centerpieces on every table. Those had to take a lot of work." Everyone claps, and I place my hand over hers. "Dinner will be served shortly, and the silent auction will open for the bidding wars to start. Thank you again, everyone, for coming. We hope you have a great evening."

Shortly after the mayor's speech, our food was brought out by the servers. We wait until we are all served before we decide to eat. You were given the choice of chicken or salmon, served with vegetables and roasted potatoes, and almost everyone at the table ordered the salmon. They have a few large tables off the side set up with different desserts you can help yourself whenever you want.

Emma and I finished eating around the same time, I asked her if she wanted dessert, but she said she wanted to dance instead. The dance floor isn't packed with people, so we make our way to it with everyone else from the table following behind us. Once we got to the dance floor, we positioned ourselves strictly as we danced in the kitchen the other night. She has her head lying against my shoulder. "Thank you for being my date tonight. Being here with you means so much to me" I look down at her. "Em, I have never been as happy as I have been with you. These last few weeks have been the best of my life, thank you."

She doesn't say anything but instead smiles at me. I know she hasn't been very open with me yet, but I hope the time is soon when she will let me know how she feels. We slow dance for a couple of songs when my mother taps my shoulder, asking for a dance. My dad doesn't seem impressed, but he puts his hand out for Emma to take so we can exchange dance partners. I take my mother's hand. "Son, I like this look on you. The look of a man very much in love. How are things going?"

I don't make eye contact with her, and I keep my eyes on my father, slow dancing with Emma, whispering something in her ear. "They are good. I can't complain. She makes me a blessed man." I can't take my eyes off them dancing, and I wish I knew what he was saying to her. I know he hasn't been fond of our relationship because of what started, but I hope he has since had a change of heart seeing us together. The song stops, so I let go of my mother and tell her we should check out the items for the silent auction.

Emma and my father see us heading that way, so they join us at the silent auction tables. We are all looking at the items silently, deciding if there is anything that we would want to bid on. It's not a guarantee that you will win that item, but if I need to pay up big for something Emma and I could use, I will do it.

I walk over to the bouquet Emma made to go with a gift card for the yearly flowers so I can see how many bids she has already had. I'm going down the list of at least ten names, and the one at the bottom is Dave Riley. I don't know what this man is doing, and I'll be damned if he wins so he can go into the shop twice a month to see Emma. I did a little quick thinking, putting down my mother's name for twice the amount Dave put on there. I know my mother has already strolled by here, so I can get away with putting down her name. She would also love the gift anyway.

I see that Emma has been standing next to the same item for a while now, so I head over to her to see what she is looking at. When I visited her, I saw that a local travel agency had donated an all-exclusive four-day trip to Sarasota, Florida. I have never seen any donation like this before, and I immediately know I need to ensure we win this. "A trip to Florida, I have never seen a donation like this, or maybe I just never noticed."

"This place isn't far from where my parents bought their retirement home before they passed. It's strange seeing pictures because I blocked this place out for so long in my mind," she frowns.

"Would you want to go? We could bid on it."

She thinks about my questions for a moment before saying, "I think we should."

When she walks away, I put down the highest bid and hope for the best.

Chapter Sixteen

Emma

This evening is turning out exactly how I thought it would. Baker was the best date, giving me all his interest and even spilling his heart on the dance floor. I wanted to express my feelings in return, and I am having difficulty figuring I feel things for him that I have never felt before, but I keep asking myself, are they real? Is this what falling for someone feels like? I have never been in the situation before, and neither has he, but he makes me seem like it's so easy with me.

I have been trying to ignore my thoughts about my feelings while enjoying the rest of the night. Jack was kind to dance with me when Catherine wanted to dance with her son. I haven't been able to figure Jack out since I met him, but he was kind while we were dancing, telling me how proud of his son he was to find someone like me. After my dance with Jack, we made our way to the auction, where I was impressed with the number of people wanting our donation. The donation of the trip to Florida took me more. Seeing pictures took me to a place I hadn't been to. I haven't seen that place in over five years, and just seeing pictures took me back to the last time I was there, for my parent's funeral. When Baker asked if I should bid on it, I couldn't say no to a place I would want to take him to one day.

Baker and I just finished piling up plates with desserts from the dessert tables and joined Ryan and Claire at the table. They announce over the microphone that bidding is closed on the items up for bid and will let everyone know later what we won. "So, did you two put bids on anything good?" I say as I bite the cheesecake I put on my plate.

"I just donated. I never really bid on anything. Claire here put a bid on a facial and massage," Ryan answered for both since Claire had her mouth full of cake.

"Sounds like something she would want to win," I laugh.

Jack and Catherine come over to the table but don't take seats. "We wanted to come to tell everyone our goodbyes. We are driving home tonight, so we must get going."

Catherine starts going around the table and hugs us, starting with Baker. She hugs me when she reaches me, "Emma, it was so good to have you here tonight. We hope you two enjoy the rest of your night."

"Thank you, Catherine. Please be safe driving. Let us know when you guys make it home."

She hugged everyone, and then she and Jack made their way to the front doors to leave.

I'm leaning back in my chair, getting tired, knowing it must be late. All of us but Baker have been sitting at the table for a while now. Ryan and Claire have had their conversation, but I have watched Baker talk to the event leader across the room for the last twenty minutes. He finally makes his way toward us, and I'm hoping he will want to head home. When he gets to the table and leans down to me, "You want to have one more dance," I look around the room. There aren't very many people left and only a few on the dance floor.

"If it's all right with you, we should head home. I am getting tired."

He kisses me, "Let's head home then."

I get up from my chair and push it in. We both tell Claire and Ryan goodbye, then Baker takes my hand, and we start heading towards the doors. Before we make it out the door, we hear someone say, "Mr. Hayes" we both turn around to see Dave Riley walking toward us.

"I just wanted to tell you it was good meeting you tonight, Emma. Baker, I'll be getting with you tomorrow. Be looking for an email. You two have a good rest of the night," he put his hand out to shake hands with him, but Baker hesitates for a second before giving him a shake.

"Thanks, Dave, have a good one," I'm too tired to ask what Dave means, so I leave it alone, and maybe he can tell me later what he meant.

When we get outside, all the setup out front has already been cleaned up. I can see Carlos standing by the car, with the door waiting for us. I slide in, and Baker gets in behind me, but he sits closer to me than usual. Once the car gets moving, he picks up my legs and lays them across his lap, resting his hand on my legs.

"Did you have fun tonight?"

I lay back against the door to relax, "Thank you for everything, getting us an invite, being my date, and making tonight amazing."

He is rubbing his palms up and down my legs, "I mean it when I said it, Emma. It means a lot to me that you came with me."

"Well, thank you." I don't know what response he wants from me.

We are silent the rest of the way home, and when his driver stops in front of the building, he opens the door for us. Baker takes my hand to help me out, and we make our way to the elevator. On the ride up to the apartment, I rest my head on Baker's shoulder while our fingers laced together, holding hands.

"We won the trip to Florida," he says quietly.

I look up at him, "We did" I'm feeling all sorts of emotions. I want to be excited and happy to show him where I am from, but inside I am a little scared about returning. Having him by my side when I go with his help eases some emotions I would have while there.

"You just tell me when you want to go, and we'll go" I squeeze his hand just as the doors open at his place.

I walk to the sofas to take a seat so I can slip my shoes off. I don't think I can take another step in these shoes. While I am taking off my shoes, Baker loosens his tie while taking a seat on the opposite sofa. "You ready for bed already?" he asks me while taking his tie off.

"I need a shower to take a quick one before bed."

He gets up and then makes his way over to help me up from the sofa. "Come on, and I'll go upstairs with you."

We get up the stairs walking into the bedroom, and I immediately want to crawl into bed, but since I'm wearing an insane amount of makeup, I need to shower. So, I head straight into the bathroom and start the shower. I leave the door open if he needs to come in to get ready for bed.

I slip my dress off, then hang it on the towel hook by the straps so I can hang it up in my closet once I shower. I get in the shower, close the door behind me and start rinsing my hair. I get shampoo, lather my hair, and then it all out. I rinse my face, standing under the water for a few minutes when I hear the door open behind me, and then feel his hands wrap around my waist, his chin resting on my shoulder, and he places a kiss right on my temple. He spins me around and places his hands on both sides of my face, then whispers, "I want you, Em," before giving me the softest kiss on my lips. I wrap my hands around his neck, bringing him closer to me, and his hands travel from my face down to my breast, where he rubs his thumbs across my nipples before his hands grip my hips. He pushes me up against the shower wall, his mouth moving down my neck and his hands staying gripped on my hips. I am trying to control my breathing with my eyes closed, resting my head against the shower wall. He whispers in my ear, "Tell me you want this. Tell me you're mine" I don't have to think about it; I want him, us. I need him to know I am serious. I take his face into my hands, locking eyes with him. "I'm yours."

He reaches over to turn the off the shower, aggressively kissing me, and then opens the shower door. He doesn't even grab towels to dry us off. We are both wet but not soaking. He picks me up, wrapping my legs around his waist, carrying me into the bedroom, and placing soft kisses along my shoulders before slowly laying me down on the side of the bed. He already has all the lamps off, and there's only light coming into the room from the shower light. Once on the bed, he spreads my legs, crawling up the bed between them. He starts with short kisses on my stomach, making his way up to my breast and then back to my lips. He's giving my body just the right amount of attention it needs before finally giving all of himself to me.

Chapter Seventeen

Baker

The further I have opened to Emma, the more I feel she is closing off me. I have expressed my emotions to her more than once and haven't received many words from her in return. I couldn't go to bed last night without knowing how she felt and letting her know I wanted her. When she got into the shower, I realized it was my shot, not only to tell her I wanted her but to show her.

I love her, and the one way I wanted to let her know was to make *love* to her. This time was nothing compared to the first time we gave ourselves to each other, and this time was so much more.

Hearing her say, "I'm yours," my heart almost burst. Those words are what I have wanted to hear for weeks. She's my girlfriend, but I want much more after those words. She makes loving her so effortless.

After making love, I held her in my arms, and as much as I wanted to tell her, "I love you," I held it in for when the time was right, and I knew when the perfect time would be to say them to her.

She's cuddled in my arms while sleeping. My arm wrapped around her while her back was up against my chest. I could stay in this bed with her all day, show her how much she means to me again, and maybe get her to open up.

I've been laying here awake, just replaying last night in my head when I hear someone come in through the door's downstairs. It's early, so I have no idea who could be showing up at an hour like this. I kiss her shoulder before slipping out of bed slowly, not waking her, grabbing a pair of shorts out of my closet and slipping them on. I turn around to check on her, she's still peacefully sleeping, and then I leave the room.

Ryan is just walking through the entryway when he says my name. I'm going down the stairs, "What are you doing here?"

"Baker, we got it!" He says, loud, while walking into the kitchen.

"Shh, keep your voice down… What are you talking about?" I make my way over to him.

"Go check your emails right now," he leans up against the kitchen counter.

I walk over to my laptop, sit on the bar stool, and open my emails. An email from Dave Riley was sent to me early this morning. I opened the email, and it was a contract for the properties.

"He wants us to buy the buildings. My plan worked. We got the girls proving to him that we were ready. We got the deal. Can you believe it? I told you this would get us exactly what we wanted."

I'm looking over the contract, not even paying attention to what Ryan says. I can't believe he sent this over this morning after trying to hit on Emma too many times last night. He is giving us a great deal on these properties, and it's a deal that we would be foolish not to take. This is going to be huge for us.

I'm still reading over the email, and Ryan says, "This means we will be rich. Girls are going to be all over us. We can travel as we have always wanted. We can let the girls get back to their normal lives, and we can move on."

I have tuned him out by the time I get to the bottom of the contract, all we need to do is sign this, and then we will officially be the biggest real estate office in New York City.

"Couldn't you have just called me about this? I don't understand why you always feel like just coming over when you want to talk. Ryan, go home, and we can talk about this later. I was up late last night, so I will return to bed for a bit; it's early. Let's meet tonight, sign this, and then we can make it official tomorrow."

He starts to the door, "Let's celebrate tonight, just the two of us."

"We can talk about this later," I wave at him as I make my way back up the stairs.

I want to spend the rest day with Emma and worry about this deal later. Once I get to the room, I notice that she is missing from the bed.

"Em," she doesn't respond, so I walk into the bathroom, look around, and she's not there.

I walk into her closet, "There you are... What are you doing"? I see her packing clothes into a bag she has placed on the ottoman. She's dressed.

"I'm leaving."

"What do you mean you are leaving"? I walk over to her to stop her from putting clothes into the bag, but she stops me with her hand on my chest from getting close.

"Don't. I have already made up my mind. I heard everything Ryan said, and I heard the whole conversation. You couldn't tell me last night about your business with Dave Riley. I now know why you didn't want to tell me anything, because you were using me," She zips up the bag, puts it over her shoulder, and then walks past me to leave.

I am following behind her, trying to remember everything Ryan said when he was here, but I was so zoned on the email that I don't remember anything.

She is rushing down the stairs in a hurry to leave, "Emma, talk to me. That isn't it at all. You have it wrong. Let me, please, explain everything to you."

"Baker, you were using me. I trusted you, and I felt betrayed in the worst way possible. I knew this would happen, and all this was too good to be true. Why didn't you tell me? You couldn't have just been honest," she stops in the entryway, and I can see tears running down her face. I want to run to her and make this better, but I need her to hear me out

"That's not true, Emma. The night I met you at the bar, Ryan sent the shots to you and Claire so that we could get you two to make us look good for Dave and close this deal. It was wrong, I know but listen, hear me out," I get closer to her. "When I took you out on our first date and got to know you, I knew it was wrong, which is why I quit talking to you. During that time, though, I thought about you every day. The deal was off when you gave me a second chance after the night at the club. I have been falling for you since. I promise I am telling the truth," I hold up my hands and hope she listens to what I just told her.

She walks towards the doors and doesn't say anything, "Emma, please. Stay. You mean everything to me, and I can't let you walk out of that door."

She stops again, turning around, and more tears fall her face. I need her to stay so I can fix this. "I'm sorry, Baker, but I can't do this" she pushes the button to open the door.

I yell out, "Em, I love you" if she walks out the door now, I will be a broken man.

She turns to me for what will be the last time, “I’m sorry, but I can’t say the same” the doors open, and she walks in. “This is goodbye, Baker.”

And just like that, she’s gone.

I start pacing the living room, thinking of anything to bring her back. I run up the stairs to grab my phone. While taking a seat on the side of the bed, I dial her number to call her. It rang once before going to voicemail. She ignored it. I call her again, and this time it doesn’t even ring, going straight to voicemail. She must have turned her phone off.

I lay back on the bed, thinking about how I had it all this morning, all I ever wanted with her, and just like that, she was gone. I should’ve told her weeks ago that I needed to be honest with her and failed. My heart breaks when I think about how I told her I loved her, and she gave me nothing in return.

I need to figure out how I can fix this, she’s the only person I have ever loved, and I want to be with her forever.

I send her one final text. I need her to see it whenever she turns her phone on.

Me: I’m sorry, Em. I was serious when I said I love you. Please, just come back to me. I’ll be waiting until then.

Chapter Eighteen

Claire

I had just gotten back to my apartment this afternoon when I got a message from Emma saying she needed me to come to her apartment and wanted to talk to me about something important. She hasn't been at her place in weeks, so I know this may have something to do with Baker.

I have missed having Emma around in the same building, and we have lost touch since the accident. It's not all her fault, mostly mine, but I don't want her to know why just yet, but I know she has been noticing something different going on with me lately.

I had just gone to the store this morning to get some sweets, so I grabbed the two pints of ice cream out of my freezer to take to her place. When we are down about something, this is always our thing, so I know this may be precisely what she needs to cheer her up.

I couldn't imagine what was happening between them, considering they were heading toward living together and probably walking down the aisle soon. I have seen how he looks at her, he loves her, and I'm honestly not surprised. I know Emma is close to coming around to loving someone, but she needs time. She has had a hard time trying to be with someone since losing her parents. I have been her friend since grade school, and never seen my best friend so broken. I have spent years with her, helping her piece herself back together, and never been so proud of the person she has become since being with Baker.

I have both pints in my hands when I open the door to her apartment.

"Emma, it's Claire," I yell out, shutting the door with my foot behind me.

"Back here," I hear her yell from her bedroom. I set the ice cream on the counter and then walked in the direction of her room. When I walked in, I could tell from her face that she had been crying for hours.

"Emma, what happened"? I climb into the bed with her and snuggle up to her while her head is on my chest. I get her hair out of her face.

"I left Baker this morning..." she can barely talk. She is crying so hard.

"It's okay. Just calm down a little, and then you can tell me everything that happened."

When she finally calms down, she tells me the whole story of how she was sleeping this morning and heard Ryan downstairs. She said she overheard Ryan discussing getting this deal secured because of us. The guys sent us shots, then used us to make themselves look better to a guy named Dave Riley. This deal will make them rich, and now they can get rid of us (strange because I don't even like Ryan) so they can vacation and get women. Whew... that's a lot of information I didn't want to know. I mean, how? I don't see Baker doing this kind of thing, but Ryan, yes, this is something he would do, no doubt.

Then she said Baker told her he loved her and didn't want her to leave, but she left because she felt betrayed by him. He told her he loves her, which isn't surprising to me because I know Baker does, but I am surprised he didn't tell her about the deal. I think he put the whole deal to the side and long forgot about it because he likes her, and I want her to realize that, but right now, I know she is in a state of shock from everything.

I talk her into moving to the couch so we can eat our ice cream while we watch *The Golden Girls* because it's another thing that makes us feel better.

"Emma, I hate that this happened to you, but I think Baker is sorry, and he didn't mean for you to find out about the deal because it wasn't anything to him anymore. Don't you love him, though?"

She takes a bite of her ice cream, thinking for a moment, "That's the thing, Claire. I was so sure last night that I was close to opening my heart up to him. Then this morning happened, and I knew when I heard what Ryan said that it's exactly why I've been hesitant, and I just wanted to leave. I just needed more time, but with this happening," she shrugs.

"I don't think you should give up on loving him because of all this mess. It would be best if you gave it another try with him. I know he loves you. I can tell by everything he does for you and when he looks at you. It makes me jealous because I want a love like that."

"Don't be jealous. It is hard to say, but I don't know if I love him. Ugh, why is this stuff so hard? I don't get why I can't just love someone so easily," she sets her ice cream down on the coffee table.

"Oh, you love him back, I know it. You need to find it in your heart that you love him."

We sit there for a few minutes watching our favorite

episode of *Golden girls*, where they win tickets to a movie premiere party with Burt Reynolds but are mistaken for prostitutes, so they end up in jail. When you think Sophia will come to their rescue to get them out, she steals their tickets. It's hilarious and couldn't have come at a better time because it has Emma laughing, even though we have seen it a hundred times.

"You want me to stay with you tonight? We haven't had a sleepover in a long time."

"Will you? I need my best friend more than anything right now," she hugs me.

We climb into bed, and I don't want to mention anything about Baker and Ryan. Ryan, mainly because that will make me think of what's making me so distant from Emma lately.

"Are you ready to get back to work tomorrow?" I know Emma loves working, and hopefully, with this stuff going on between her and Baker, she will be fine working tomorrow.

"You know I won't let this interfere with work. We will have fun tomorrow just like we always do," Emma turns her face towards me while talking to me.

I smile at her, and then she reaches over to her nightstand to turn off the lamp. We both cuddle up on our pillows and go to sleep like other times we have needed each other for a sleepover.

I'm running from a guy dressed in black with a bat as fast as I can, and Ryan is standing at the other end, yelling for me to run faster so he can save me. The guy dressed in black catches up to me and throws me to the ground. He holds me down with his hands while I fight him off me. I'm screaming and fighting for my life when I finally grab his mask with one hand, trying to rip it off his face so I can see who it is. Before I can pull it off, he slaps me across the face, and then it goes black. Ryan is still yelling for me to come to him in the background...

I wake up sweating from the reoccurring dream I have had since the accident. I sit straight up in the bed, breathing heavily, and look over to see that Emma is still sleeping. The clock on her side table reads *five thirty am.*

Laying back down, I pull the covers back up over my shoulders. I have been having this dream at the same time every night, and I know it's been because I have been hiding a secret from my best friend, and I haven't held a secret from Emma since the time I once had a crush on the same boy in ninth grade as her. I need to tell her. I make myself comfortable again and then close my eyes to try to fall back to sleep.

I wake up to the smell of coffee and roll over to see that Emma is already out of bed this morning. I get up and make my way to the kitchen. Emma is pouring a cup of coffee, still wearing the clothes she slept in, so it must still be early. "Hey, I made coffee if you wanted to take some with you before you go to your place to get ready"? she seems good this morning, which is probably the perfect time for me to shoot my shot.

"Thank you, Emma." I go to the cabinet to grab a mug and then pour myself some.

When I turn around, she's leaning against the counter, taking a sip from her mug.

"There might be something I need to tell you. I have been hiding something from you."

Chapter Nineteen

Baker

These last two days have been the longest two days of my life. I haven't heard from Emma, and she must have blocked me because none of my texts or calls have been going through to her. I told myself I would wait and let her come around, but after just a couple of hours, I found myself on my phone trying to get in touch with her.

My apartment reminds me of her, and I can't make coffee without wondering if she's sometimes drinking. I made some for her. I get ready in the bathroom and look in her closet, wishing she was there so I could help her pick what to wear. I have been using the extra shower because mine takes me back to the other night we were together. The worst is going to bed alone, smelling her on the sheets, and using her pillow to fall asleep because I miss her so much it hurts.

I went into the office to work yesterday but left for a run before noon, and I never went back in after my run. Ryan has been bothering me to sign my name to the contract Dave Riley worked up for the deal, but I can't get myself to sign my name to something so big when I'm going through this right now. I told Ryan to give me until the end of the week to work my issues out, and then I can decide if I want to do this. He isn't happy with me right now, but it's just because he doesn't understand.

A few times, I check in on the cameras at the flower shop just so I can see her and know that she is safe, but I haven't seen her. I don't know if she isn't there or has been in the back office. Claire is always working the counter while the two new girls have been working on arrangements.

The doors open to my place, and I'm instantly feeling miserable. Instead of joining Emma at the kitchen island and eating the dinner she just made for us, I am going upstairs to change out of my work clothes and into my running clothes so I can ease my mind. I need to find the courage and try to get over this or figure out a way to get her back. I need to do both, try to figure out my life while trying to get her back.

I had just tied up my running shoes when I heard the doors open downstairs. I know it is Ryan, and I'm sure he wants me to close this deal with Dave already. I yell, give me a minute, and then I take a deep breath. I leave the bedroom doorway to find Claire and Ryan sitting on the sofas in the living room.

I don't understand what they are doing together. Does this have something to do with Emma?

"What's going on? Is Emma okay? Why are both of you here?" Claire is frowning. This can't be good. They both confused me so much that I didn't even take a seat. I stand next to the couch.

"We have something we need to tell you. It has to do with Emma," Ryan says.

I start pacing the living room, sweating. "What?"

Claire sits up, "Since this is my problem, I'll be the one to tell you..." she pauses, making me even more nervous.

"Come on you two. What the hell is going on?"

"Okay, the accident at the shop was my fault," Claire says,

tears welling up in her eyes.

"Your fault. What do you mean? They never found the guy who robs the place, so what do you mean it's your fault."

Ryan finally says, "Claire's ex-boyfriend James was the guy who robbed the shop, and he hurt Emma more than what Claire said that night."

"The night the shop got robbed. I had this feeling that I knew who it was who did it. I started having these dreams, and then it came to me one day that I knew it had to be James. We broke up the day after meeting you two. He never liked Emma because he always thought she was trying to keep me away from him. He started sending me threatening calls and text messages before breaking into the flower shop...."

Ryan interrupts Claire, "Baker, he took the bat to more than just Emma's head. She is fortunate she survived. Claire came to me a couple of days after the accident and asked me to help her catch him. So, I did because she knew you'd try to kill him if she told you. We had enough evidence from phone records and cameras from neighboring businesses to prove to the cops it was him, and just a few days ago, we caught him trying to hide in the car shop he works. We got him and have enough evidence to lock him up for a long time."

I take a seat, trying to process everything they just told me. "We need to go to Emma. She needs to know all of this."

Claire is sitting there with a sad face, "She already knows."

"What, When? She didn't tell me anything, and this is something she would've told me."

"I told her Monday morning. I stayed with her Sunday because of everything going on with you and her. I woke up during the night with another nightmare of the accident and knew I needed to tell her I had been keeping a secret. I knew it probably wasn't the best time, but I needed to tell her. She's gone, Baker. She left town."

"Great, so you're telling me she left town because the two people she should've trusted more than anyone betrayed her" I rub my hands down my face and then get up from the couch. "We need to find her, like right now. We need to fix what we did to her because she doesn't deserve this. She deserves better."

"I've already tried looking for her, and I don't know where she is. After I told her about all this, she seemed fine, so I went to my apartment to get ready for work so we could go in together. When I returned to her place, the door was locked, and there was a note saying she had left town for the week and would be back on Monday. She didn't say where she was going or leave any clues."

"Does she have any family back in Florida she could be staying with?" I pace the living room again, trying to think of where she could be.

"No, after her parents passed away, the only family she had left moved away, and she hasn't been in touch with any of them. I don't think she went to Florida, either. That's not a place she would go if she were upset."

"She hasn't been answering me, so I'm unable to get in touch with her. If you hear from her, will you please let me know? I need to know she's okay."

The room gets quiet for a moment. We are all trying to process this mess and where she could have gone.

"Baker, maybe she needs this time away for herself. She is going through so many things right now. She said she would be back on Monday, so let's see what happens when she returns. She hates both of us, so that will give us the rest of the week to figure out the best way to apologize to her."

I don't want to do what Claire says, but she's right; we need to give her space to think about things. I don't want her to say goodbye to me. I don't want to think she doesn't want to come back to me while she is thinking through all this.

"Look, this is hard to say, but maybe you're right. We need to let her think through this without us. I wish I knew where she was so I know she is fine."

"She will come back to you, Baker, I know it. She needs time, but I know she will love you," Claire says while giving me a grin, and I smile back because I hope she is right.

Claire gets up from the couch and goes to the entryway. Ryan joins her so they can leave together. "Is there something going on between you two"?

They look at each other with a disgusting face, "No way, we are just friends," Claire says, and Ryan shakes his head to agree.

I laugh, "Thank you for coming to tell me all of this. You two did a great job getting this James guy, and you're right too... I would've killed him. If you hear anything from her, Claire, I'm serious when I say let me know."

"I promise I will tell you," Then they get in the elevator to leave.

I forget about going for a run and instead lay across the couch, thinking about what happened to her. That night during the break-in, I'm so glad she doesn't remember anything from that night.

I desperately want to be there for her and comfort her during this time. When her parents passed, she leaned on Claire for so long to be there for her, and now it breaks me to know she is alone during this time, but she needs her space, as Claire said.

I lay on the couch, thinking about her for a while, deciding to get some rest. The days will go by quicker if I stick to my work and home schedule during the week and then come up with something to do over the weekend. I must focus on staying busy and not thinking about anything terrible with Emma. Monday will be here before we know it, she will be back in town, and I can focus then on how to get her back.

When I get into bed, I do the same thing I have done the past two nights. I grab Emma's pillow and sleep with it, knowing that's the closest I'm going to get to her for the night.

Chapter Twenty

Baker

It's Friday, and we are just a few days away from Emma back in town, and I would say the week has been going by quickly. Since Ryan and Claire spilled the news the other night, I have been getting up, going to work, and running errands, then when I get home, I go for a run, followed by dinner all alone at the kitchen island, and then I go straight to bed while watching episodes of shows I would watch with her. I called my mom yesterday to confirm that they would be home this weekend so that I could stay there so I wouldn't have to stay in this empty apartment alone, and maybe my mom could give me some advice on getting her back. When I talked to my mother to ask her about this weekend, I lied to her telling her Emma would be away for a girl's weekend with Claire so she wouldn't wonder where she would be. I don't want my parents to know what has been going on until I get there, and we can talk about it in person.

I met up with a client for lunch today, so I could take care of some business and eat instead of another meal by myself. Who knew that something like that would bother me after being alone and doing it for so long? I didn't realize how much she had changed me until she was gone.

When I return to my office after lunch, there's a big envelope on my desk waiting for me, but instead of just my name on the front, it says Baker Hayes and Emma Adler. I take a seat to open the letter, thinking maybe it's something she sent to me while she was away but instead, I pull out prints of the pictures taken of us during the charity ball. I flip through them. There's one of us before we stop, and a few of us with her hand on my chest. I flip through them some more, and the last picture is of me giving her *a look*, with my hand holding her chin up, and she's smiling at me. Just looking at it stops me because you can tell we are two people in love in the picture. While this would be the perfect picture of us for the paper as an official couple, it never made the front paper like I thought it would. The newspaper instead printed a photo of Ryan and Claire on the front page with the title *New couple alert*. I laughed when I saw it, not because it wasn't the picture of Emma like it and I thought, but because Ryan and Claire aren't even a couple.

I put the photos of us back inside the envelope, leaving out the last picture on my desk. I have plans for that one. I opened my phone and wanted to send Emma the picture, but I knew it'd be too much, so instead, I tried to send her a text. I want to see if she has me blocked still. I open our messages,

Me: There has not been a day gone by that I haven't thought about you, Em. I miss you...

The arrow is blue instead of green, meaning I'm not blocked anymore, so I hit send, and I hope she gets it and sends me a reply. I want to hear from her.

I wait a few minutes, and nothing, so I just put my phone down and get back to some work so I can get out of here to pack a bag for the weekend and the drive out to the Hamptons.

It's been an hour or so, and my phone pings with an alert.

My heart races when I pick up my phone, but all it says is Emma liked your text. It wasn't a reply, but it was something. I know she got it, and that's all that matters. The fact that she unblocked me was enough to put a smile on my face.

When I walk out of the office, I feel better than I have had all week. Emma got my message, and I'm just a couple of days away from being able to see her. She may not want to see me in person then, but I know she will be back at the shop, and I can eavesdrop on her there. I decide to make one quick stop before heading home.

I pull up outside the flower shop and park my car. I haven't been here in a while, but I figured I would check in with Claire, letting her know I would be out of town this weekend and see if she has heard anything from Emma. I walk up to the front door, open it, and I get this feeling that maybe Emma may be here, but once I walk in, it's just Claire at the front desk.

"Hey," she says when she sees me walking in.

I walk over to the front counter, resting my elbows. "Have you heard anything from Emma all at?"

She frowns, "Nope, nothing. I tried to text her, but she never responded. I think she must be pretty mad at us for not even check-in in, or she's somewhere where she is comfortable, and she's just busy."

"I'm going to go with she's mad at us," I laugh.

"I think you are right. So, what are you doing here if you know she isn't here?"

"I want to see if you have heard from her. I sent her a message today to see if I could get in touch with her, and she liked my message, so it's something, but I wanted to let you know that I'll be at my parent's for the weekend. If she comes back to town early, will you let me know? I'll only be a few hours away if I need to come back."

"I will be in touch if anything happens, but I don't think we will see her till Monday. I think she needed the time away."

I have the envelope in my hands, and I lay it down, sliding it over to Claire, "Will you do me a favor and leave these on her desk for when she gets back? They are the photos from the Charity Gala."

She picks up the envelope and smiles. "I can do that for you."

I stand up, getting ready to leave. "Thanks, Claire. I will see you sometime next week."

She yells, "Bye, Baker," while I walk to the door.

I'm at my apartment packing my bag to get ready to leave when I hear Ryan's voice calling my name. I go out the door, then downstairs, "What do you want now? I'm just getting ready to leave for the weekend."

He's sitting on the couch, "I just wanted to come by before you left town. I hoped we could meet with Dave and take care of business."

I sit opposite him, resting against the back of the couch, my arms across my chest, "I'm sorry, Ryan, but I can't take the deal."

He gets up immediately and starts pacing the room. "What, are you crazy? We have to take that deal, Baker."

"I know, but I can't do it. I know it means a lot to you, and we could get a ton of benefits from it, but I think it just feels wrong to do something that will take up my time from her and why she left me."

He's pacing and shaking his head. "Seriously?"

"I'm serious. We are already so successful, Ryan. I know we will be just fine letting go of this deal. She means more to me than making money off these buildings, and if I want to get her back, I can't do it, and I am more than okay with that."

He stops with his hands on his sides. "If that is what you want to do, then I guess I will have to trust that we are making the right decision. I have trusted you with making choices for our company all these years, and I know how much Emma means to you."

"Thank you for understanding, Ryan. I'll send Dave an email this weekend to let him know. You want to come with me this weekend to stay at Mom and Dad's?"

He sits on the couch, "I'm going to pass on that. Staying here is what I would like to do this weekend."

"I won't leave for another hour if you change your mind. The plan is to have a relaxing weekend while they take care of some stuff in town."

"Tempting, but I'll stay. I know you could use the weekend to yourself. You have some things you need to think about," Ryan gets up from the couch to leave.

"Thank you again for understanding. I'll be back in the office Monday," I get up to head back upstairs to finish packing. "Don't get into trouble this weekend while I'm gone."

"You don't worry about me. I'll be fine. See you Monday."

I pull up outside my parent's house, it looks like no one is home, so I grab my bag from the back seat and then head for the front door, unlocking it with my key. I walk inside to a few lamps my mother probably left on so I could see when I got here. I walk around to ensure no one's here and set my bag on the couch.

Once I make sure no one is around, I walk outside on the back patio to relax on the lounge chairs until my parents return from wherever they are. I take a seat and lay back with my hand on my chest. It's dark outside, the sky lit with the stars, and it takes me back to the night I had asked her to be my girlfriend officially. I close my eyes, and I can see her smile on her face and laughing the night we were in the park. I don't imagine her for long before my parents interrupt me from my thoughts.

"Baker, how long have you been here"? My mother says, coming up and hugging me before sitting next to me on the lounge chair.

"Just a few minutes. Where have you two been"? My father is in the kitchen warming up some food to eat.

"We just had some things to do in town before you got here. I hope it's okay with you, but our weekend plans got canceled, so we will be here during your stay. We will try to stay out of your way if you'd like us to."

I plan on relaxing by the pool and taking a run by the ocean, but I don't have a problem having them around. I could use some advice from my mother, but I don't intend to tell her what happened between Emma and me just yet.

"No, I don't mind at all."

“Well, good dear, Are you hungry or anything? We haven’t eaten, and your father is heating some leftovers from last night.”

“I’m good, mom, thanks for asking, but I think I will just hang out here for a little longer before heading to bed,” She gets up from the lounge chair and heads into the kitchen.

I slide my phone out of my shorts pocket. Dave played an ugly game with me at the charity event before he gave us the buildings. I called my father a few days ago for some advice about the deal and told him then I wouldn’t be doing it, so I know he may be upset with me this weekend.

After sending the email and checking for any missed messages, I decide I should call it a night, so I head into the kitchen to find my parents still at the table in a deep conversation that ends as soon as I walk into the room. I don’t know what they had to eat for dinner, but it smells incredible, familiar.

I walk by them without saying anything so they can return to their conversation and head upstairs. My parent’s home isn’t the home I grew up in, but they have a room set up for each of us to stay in when we visit. The room they have set up for me is decorated to match the rest of the house and holds some of my childhood things on a small shelf. When I enter the room, I examine the shelf, which holds a couple of trophies from when I played baseball in high school, some photos of me playing baseball, and then a photo of me in uniform with my parents. I haven’t stayed here in a while for the weekend, and I have only been coming for dinner and then heading back home. I fall onto the bed, lounging my head back on the pillow, and then put my hands behind my head. It’s not that late, but I’m tired, so it doesn’t surprise me when my eyes start closing on me before I can even turn the lights off in the bedroom.

When I wake up the next day, I feel rested, as if I slept in my bed at home. I headed downstairs for a drink of water and was greeted by both of my parents in the kitchen. They don't say anything to me as they make their coffee and chat about the weather. I open the fridge and find some leftover containers. "Do you happen to have any water?"

"There should be some at the back of the fridge, son," my father says while taking a sip of his coffee at the kitchen island.

I move over some containers, one of which looks like leftover lasagna, and I finally find a few water bottles at the back. I grab one, then shut the fridge door. Both of my parents are quiet now. "So, what is the plan for today, Baker?"

"I think I'm going to go for a run, then spend some time in the pool," I say, opening the water to take a drink while standing in front of the fridge.

My father nods and returns to drinking his coffee while my mother stays silent. They haven't asked about Emma, which is odd. My mother brings her up almost every time I talk to her on the phone. I will continue to act as if nothing has been going wrong with our relationship with them. I walk into the living room to head back upstairs when I realize the flowers in the entryway are like the one Emma had made my mother once before. When she made the arrangements, they were made with whites, which are the same but with red, and I don't remember Emma mentioning making flowers for my mother again. She probably just had the local flower shop match the arrangements that she had made for her.

I walk into the room and lie down to check some emails before heading out for a beach run. Just as I lay back on the bed, it all comes to me—the smell of the bed, the leftovers in the fridge, and the flowers. I get up, but this time I run downstairs, and when I enter the kitchen, my parents are staring at me, "Where is she? She was here, wasn't she?"

They look at each other a look before turning back to me, "What are you talking about?" my mother says as she starts wiping the clean kitchen counter with a towel.

"Emma, she was here. You two know what happened and didn't even say anything to me. You didn't tell me she was here?"

"Baker, listen... She didn't want you to know she was here. She didn't want us to know something was going on between you. I brought her here, and she just needed some time for herself. We drove her back yesterday when she found out you were coming here. She felt it was best she left so that you could come here to clear your mind," my mother finally says.

I sit on the kitchen bar stool, rest my elbows on the counter, and then rub my hands down my face. I don't even know what to say, but I have many questions. Why did she come here from all the places, and what did she say there?

Chapter Twenty-one

Emma

Five days earlier…

"There's something I need to tell you; I have been hiding something from you," Claire says just as I take a sip from my mug.

"Does this have something to do with why you have been acting weird lately? Because if so, let me sit down for this because you never hide anything of me," I make my way over to the couch while she pours herself a mug of coffee and then takes a seat next to me.

Once she takes a seat, she takes a deep breath and then turns to me. "Emma, I love you, and you know I do, so what I am about to say will upset you, but I want you to know that I did it because I care about you so much."

I don't say anything, and I shake my head so she can continue with what she needs to tell me.

"James was the man who broke into the flower shop. I didn't know until after the accident that he could do something like this. James sent me threatening messages before the break-in and told me he would pay you for breaking us up. I didn't think he would do anything, so I told him to stop messaging me and move on with his life. Then after the accident, I started having these vivid dreams that he was the man in the mask, and when I realized the messages had stopped, I thought it had to be him. I didn't want you or Baker involved because it was my problem, so I asked Ryan to help me. So, some nights we tracked James to make sure it was him before we took the evidence to the police station, and sure enough, after following him for a few days, we were right. We caught him talking about it to his friends, and the police found evidence on his phone and at his house."

I don't even know what to say. I lay my head against the couch and watch her finish what she has to say.

"Emma, this is all my fault, and I am so sorry. He could have killed you. I didn't want to say anything to anyone, but that night when I ran out after you screamed, I saw him hit you more than what I told you, then you fell, and that's when he hit you over the head. I knew I needed to fight him away to save you." She starts crying, so I grab her hand to tell her it's okay.

"The dreams stopped when we caught him, and then I had one last night. I knew I needed to tell you to stop the nightmares. I have kept this bottled up every night since the accident because I knew it would hurt you. I know this isn't the right time to say anything because of all this stuff between you and Baker, but I needed to tell you. I'm sorry that I lied to you, and I know Baker is sorry for keeping a secret from you too. I love you, Emma, and I'm truly sorry."

I squeeze her hand. I'm not even sure what to say right now. It hurts that the people who love me have kept secrets, but I need to remind myself they did it to protect me. I don't want her to see any tears, I have cried enough from Baker, and I don't want to show Claire that she caused any more.

"Listen, Claire, how about we talk about this later? We

both need to get to work, so why don't we get ready for the day, and we can walk to work together? Then tonight, we can open a bottle of wine, order some pizza, and discuss this. Just know that I understand. I love you, and thank you for protecting me," I hug her before we both get up from the couch.

She grabs her bag from the night before out of my room. Then goes to the front door to leave but turns to me. "I'll be back so we can walk to work. Thanks for listening, Emma. I feel relieved now that I told you."

"I'll see you soon," I say as she opens the door and walks out. Then the door shuts. I walk over to it to lock it and then head to the bathroom to get ready for work.

The tears start falling down my face before I even enter the bathroom. I start the shower and then stand in front of the mirror. I already look like a mess. These last couple of days have been the worst. Not as bad as losing my parents, but it comes close. The two people I trusted more than anyone kept things from me that I should have known. Before I take my clothes off, I hear my phone ringing, so without thinking, I pick up my phone off the nightstand to see that Catherine is calling me.

I try my hardest to hold back my tears, so she won't ask me if anything is wrong, but when I answer the phone, she can immediately tell.

"Hello, Catherine," tears coming back down

"Emma… honey, is everything alright?"

I wipe my face and then put my head down. "I want to say yes, but everything is not okay, Catherine. I'm so sorry, but I shouldn't have answered. Right now is not a good time."

"Oh dear, where are you? I'm on my way to come to get you," she sounds like she's in the car.

"Catherine, there's no need for that. I think I will be okay once I get to work," I look out my bedroom window watching the traffic.

"Emma, you do not sound okay. You don't have to tell me what you are going through now. You can come to go back home with me today. Tell Claire and Baker you need a few days off work."

I do not get how she knows what I need without even asking. It is because she's a mom, making me miss my own at this time. I know she is right, though. I need to get out of here so I can clear my head. I don't even stop her, and I get up to look for a bag. I tell her to meet me right out front of my apartment building, and then I hang up the phone. I write a note to put on my front door for Claire, and then I get into the shower and hope I can make it before Claire makes her way back to my apartment.

I'm in such a rush that once I am out of the shower, I get dressed quickly and then throw clothes into a bag that should last me a few days. After grabbing anything else I know I would need, I make my way downstairs to the front entrance of my apartment building. Catherine is already waiting for me when I walk out the front doors.

I open the front passenger side door and get into the car. "Thank you for doing this, but I want you to know that you didn't have to."

"Emma dear, it doesn't bother me one bit. I don't know what is going on with you, but I would love to spend some time with you. You deserve a few days off, and I know Baker and Claire will not mind. We do not have to talk about anything at all," She says while driving off into traffic.

"Why did you come into town today?"

"I came into town to see you. I was going to see if you could make me some arrangements for the house and then see what plans you had for the rest of the day. I know it is a Monday, but I was hoping we could get some time together. It looks like we will get some girl time today, just not as I had planned."

I love that she wants to spend time with me, getting to know me better, but I don't want to ruin this time with her by telling her what has been happening between me and Baker the last couple of days. I can make this time with her outstanding by taking my mind off everything and doing enjoyable stuff with her. I would want my mother during this time, so I know I could use her to help me take my mind off all my unhappiness.

"When we get into town, I can gather flowers from local stores and work together on making arrangements. It will be fun working together."

She smiles at me and then turns her attention back to driving.

We both spend the next couple hours of the drive primarily quiet, only talking about what we could do while I stay. When we get into town, we stop for flowers, letting Catherine pick what flowers she wants to use. It is no surprise when she picks red roses, considering they always remind me of love. Jack greets us when we pull up the driveway to their wonderful home. He is standing out front, watering the gorgeous landscaping they have. When I get out of the car with Catherine, he gets a confused look, and I know it is because he was not expecting me to be there.

"Jack, Emma will stay with us for a couple of days. I knew we could use some girl time, so I asked her to come to stay with us."

I know she protects me and does not want him to know why I am staying with them.

Jack does not even come over to us. He waves and then goes back to watering the landscaping. I am beginning to think he does not like me, so I will stay out of his way while I am here.

Once we are inside, I feel relief because this place feels like the home I shared with my parents. I make my way up to stairs and pick Baker's room to stay in while I am here. I put my bag down on the bed before checking out the stuff in the room. I found some old photos of him with his parents on a shelf from what looks like high school when he played baseball. He doesn't look much different than he did then, and looking at the photo makes me miss him so much. My phone comes through with a text while I look at the trophies on the shelf. I walk over to my bag and pull my phone out so I can see who it is

Claire: I am so sorry, Emma. Just let me know that you are safe

I read the message and then contemplated messaging her back. I read the message several times before sticking it back into my bag.

I take to sit on the side of the bed. Then I lay on the pillow with my hands over each other on my chest. I think about how I got here. Of all the places I could be right now during a time like this, I never once thought I would end up at Baker's parents' house. Catherine has been friendly to me since the day I met her, and I know she relates to me as a person because we seem to have gone through the same thing in our lives, losing our parents at an early age. I know that she may think that might be why I was upset, that I was having a day because I know I have had plenty of those days since I lost my parents, but it is not. I do not intend to bring Baker up to her because he has been amazing to me, but she does not need to know about the deal, and it is not my place to tell her.

I get up from the bed and go downstairs to the kitchen, where I find Catherine making us something for lunch.

"There you are. I was about to get you. I made us sandwiches for lunch. We can eat on the patio out back together, or you can take it back upstairs?" She picks up two plates with sandwiches.

"Thank you, Catherine, but I would love to join you on the patio," I help her with the plates, and she walks to the fridge to grab two lemonades.

We make our way outside to the dining table on the back patio taking seats across from each other. The weather today is beautiful, and while we both start eating our sandwiches, I think I should go for a walk along the beach later.

"After lunch, would you like to work on those flower arrangements? I can teach you all secrets, and one day you will be able to make your own," I say, interrupting our silence.

"I would love that, Emma," she smiles at me before taking a sip of her lemonade and then setting it down. "I don't want to intrude, and I know I said I didn't want to know what is going on, but I do want to know if you are doing okay." She pushes her plate to the side and rests her hands on her lap.

I push my plate over, "I'm doing as good as I can right now. I don't want to say much, but the last couple of days have been hard, and I know being here right now is just what I need to help get my mind back on track. Thank you for bringing me here when you do not even know what I am going through. I am still unsure why I answered your call while crying, but I am glad I did."

"I want to be here for you, dear. We have not known each other long, but I want you to be able to come to me if you ever need anything. My son has done a lot for you, but sometimes you need a mother figure to help you get through the tough stuff. I went through many trials when I was younger, and I never had anyone but Jack to look to when I needed help. I know you will need someone besides Baker or Claire, and I want you to know you can depend on me to be that person, even if what you are going through has to do with my son."

"I do appreciate it, Catherine… Thank you," I lean back in my chair and stare out onto the ocean, thinking I did not deserve such wonderful people as the Hayes family.

Catherine gets up and hugs me and then gathers our plates to take back inside. "Just come in whenever you are ready."

I think to myself about how I got here. I was just a girl who happened to be at the right spot at the right time. It was not Baker who picked us that night. It was Ryan, and then Baker just chose me. When we went on our first date, I thought he was interested, but he was leading me on to help get a deal. Then I went a couple of weeks without hearing from him because he did have feelings, only to find him knock a guy out at the club. I gave him another chance, only for him to fall in love with me. While I want my heart to be ready to love Baker, I need a sign telling me that this is what I want. What he did was wrong, but I know he is remorseful for protecting me, just like Claire did by not telling me everything I needed to know. I need to use these few days to slow down my life so that I can get a clearer picture of what I want my future to hold. The relationship between Baker and I was moving so quickly that this time away from each other was just what we both needed to make sure this was what we both wanted.

I spent the rest of my first night with Catherine, putting together the arrangements, and I even kept her company in the kitchen while she made us dinner. Jack never made another appearance except for when dinner was ready. He came down from his office, where I know he was almost all day, and joined us to eat, then went back upstairs. Catherine portrayed it as if it were something he does every night. After I helped her clean up the mess in the kitchen, we said our goodnights before I went upstairs to my room to get rest.

Before I get into bed for the night, I pull my phone out of my bag to check it one more time and unblock Baker because I want to know if he is trying to get in touch with me, I miss him, and I could use a message from him right now. I never responded to Claire, and I will wait until I get back into town so I can talk to her in person.

I have been here for days, and it has been precisely what I needed. We do not talk about anything but what is going on in the moment. Catherine had graced me with stories of Baker from when he was a young boy. These are the kind of stories that I will not be repeating to him once I see him again.

I spent the last few days hanging out by the pool, thinking about life, and just trying to have a fun time. Catherine has been excellent and has given me the space I needed during my time here. We have gotten to know each other better while I have been here, and having a mom around has been a great feeling. She reminds me so much of my mother. Jack was not around me during my stay, only for dinner every night.

Baker called yesterday and told his parents he would be coming down Friday to stay the weekend with them, and it brought a smile to my face just hearing from him, even though he did not speak to me personally.

Since tonight is my last night, I told Catherine I would make them dinner this evening. She insisted I make my lasagna because she said Baker raved about it being so good. We went into town earlier to grab the ingredients for dinner, and now that we are back, I decided I would like to take a walk along the beach before we start dinner.

After walking for a little while, I sit in the sand and take in the sunset view with the wind blowing through my hair when I hear a voice come up behind me.

"Care if I join you?"

The voice sounds familiar, and when I turn around, there stands Jack. He would be the last person I suspected to join me. I turn back around and pat the sand next to me for him to take a seat. He sits with me and sits silently for just a moment.

We are both watching the sunset when he finally breaks the silence. "I want to talk to you about something." I continue to stare out at the ocean, "Go ahead."

He clears his throat, "I want you to know that I know what happened between you and my son. He did not tell me anything; I just put what was going on together. I want you to know that I knew about the deal with him and Ryan, and you found out about it, which is why you are here."

I finally look at him, "You all knew, and no one thought to tell me anything about it?" I shake my head.

"Catherine doesn't know. When Baker brought you here that night to meet us, he told me that the deal was off with Ryan and that he was falling for you," he pauses. "My son loves you, and I know this because he called me yesterday for some advice about this deal with Dave Riley. When I told him to do what he wanted, he told me he was not taking it. If you had to ask me, he is not taking it because his love for you is greater than making money off this,"

A tear falls down my cheek, he is not taking the deal, and at this moment, I realize that means so much to me. During this escape, I completely forgot what he would do about this chaos, and his father answered that for me. The thought of me meant more to him than taking this deal makes my heart so pleased.

Jack puts his arm around me and brings me into a side hug. "I want you to know, Emma, at first, with you being here, I was upset at my son for bringing you to us through such bad circumstances, and then today, when I talked to him, he sounded not himself. I knew then that you were here for a reason and because of him. I want the two of you to make this right. I know you love each other and will forget all about this over time. Catherine and I could not be happier to have someone like you in this family. You have brought not only my son so much joy but to my wife. She finally found someone who connects with her on a level we cannot. So, I know in my heart that Baker is deeply sorry for what he has done, and I hope you two can make this work."

I put my arm around him, hugging him back while I still have tears. "Thank you so much, Jack… and here I didn't think you liked me," I wipe the tears from my cheek.

"Emma, I have been distant with you because of all this with Baker and Ryan. It made me so angry thinking they went this low to make money, but now that I know the truth, I will never be the same to you. I am proud of my son for realizing the person you were and letting this go for you. This is a first for me, and I have never been pleased they didn't take a deal with work before," he laughs.

We both stand up, and I dust the sand off myself before we start walking back to the house. "I am so thankful for you, Jack. I want you to know that I genuinely love your son, and my time here away from him has taught me that. I have guarded my heart against him because of what I have gone through, but he makes me complete. I have held back from loving him, and my time away from him made me realize that he is exactly the person I need in my life."

As we walk back, he puts his arm around my shoulders, "I'm happy to hear that. Now all you two need is a fresh start with each other and forget about this whole mess."

I smile, "I think I have the perfect plan for that."

Tonight's dinner at their house was the best. Jack and Catherine helped me cook, and we all went in together to clean the kitchen. When we finished, we took the bottle of wine, opened outside to the dining table on the patio, and sat the rest of the evening, just enjoying the night under the stars. Catherine is happy to have Jack with us tonight, and I wish Baker were here to enjoy this moment with us.

Tomorrow they will take me back to the city, and Baker should arrive here tomorrow night. I could stay till he gets here, but I know he could use a heart-to-heart with his father just like I did. I never expected Jack to be the person to make me feel better in this whole situation, but just my conversation with him today healed the way my heart was feeling.

It was getting late, so we all headed to our rooms for the night. I have been lying in bed, tossing for a couple of hours, trying to go to sleep, but I have been thinking about how I will tell Baker my feelings for him. He has done many beautiful things for me, and I want to make this moment special for both of us, something to remember.

Chapter Twenty-two

Emma

"Morning, Catherine" I sit up from the bed, rubbing my eyes so they can adjust to the sunlight from her opening the curtains.

She grabs my hand after she sits me down by me on the bed. "Emma, before we go, I want you to know that you are welcome to come back here anytime you want to. Just let me know if you ever need anything. Also, you can call me Mom if you would like. Everyone around her calls me mom, and I think you should be able to call me that, too," she smiles.

I wrap my hand around our hands and hold them. "I would like that, thank you."

We embrace each other before she gets up from the bed to leave the room. I pull the covers off me and get up from the bed. I look at myself in the mirror that hangs above the dresser. I look pleasantly well for not getting sleep, and I smile at the thought of returning home today. My time here has ended, and I want to make things right with Claire when I get back into town and stop by the shop and check on things. I miss that place.

After getting ready and devouring the best pancakes anyone has ever made me, we headed back into the city. They dropped me off at my apartment, and after giving both a goodbye with promises of seeing them again very soon, I headed inside.

Claire is still working at the flower shop for the day, so I couldn't stop by her apartment to talk about everything. I head to my apartment instead, deciding to talk to her later today and see if she would like to come by after work.

I open the door to my apartment, and while it does not feel like home like Baker's place feels, I still am happy to be here. I walk inside, close the door behind me and walk straight down the hallway to my bedroom. I throw my bag in front of the closet door and then fall onto the bed. I could sleep from all the excitement from the week, but I just lay there looking up at the ceiling, thinking about how good it felt to figure out what I wanted to do finally. I hear my phone ping with a notification from my bag on the floor. I get up from the bed and take my phone out from the side pocket of my bag to find a message

Baker: There has not been a day gone by that I have not thought about you, Em. I miss you...

I want to tell him so badly I miss him, and I want to see him and hug him, but I cannot do that. I have a plan, and I know he will visit his parents tonight. I shower to pass the time, and I will at least let him know once I finish getting ready that I got his message.

It is closing time at the flower shop, and I am standing out front of the shop looking up at the billboard of Baker and Ryan, about to head inside to talk to Claire. Taken back to the day the billboard was up, and how I used to despise these two, it is crazy how far life has come since that day.

I walk into the shop to find Claire sweeping the floors like she always does. "Hey," she turns to me with a massive grin. "I've missed you, Emma," then she runs over to me, hugging me.

I wrap my arms around her in a big embrace. "I've missed you too."

"Where have you been? Tell me everything," she walks over to the front counter, follows behind her, and takes a seat on the stool.

"Well... I've been with Catherine and Jack. Shortly after you left my apartment on Monday, Catherine called me and could tell I was upset about something, so she told me to pack a bag. She picked me up, and they brought me back this afternoon. They could tell I needed some space, so they let me relax at their house for a few days. It was just what I didn't know I needed," I tell her while leaning against the counter.

"That's great, Emma, not where I thought you were. I would have never expected you to be at his parents' house. Does he know you were there? Do they know what happened between the two of you and us?" she motions her hand between them.

"No, they do not know anything about us, but Jack knows what happened between Baker and me. I didn't tell him. He just figured it out himself. He knew about the idea Ryan produced for them to get this deal, and when Baker called him the other day to tell him he was not taking the deal, he knew something had to happen between us for him not to take it. He and I had a conversation on the beach the other day, and he helped me realize some things."

Claire's face shows that she is shocked to hear that Jack and I talked, he hasn't been the friendliest person during my time of knowing him, but after talking with him on the beach, he has a special place in my heart.

"Wow, Jack? He has seemed so distant the whole time you have seen Baker."

"He has been that way because he was upset with the guys about the deal. It was not because he did not like me; he did not like how Baker met me. He knew the whole thing was wrong, and someone would get hurt. He told me that Baker told him the deal was off weeks ago and that he was falling for me. Now that this is out there, he told me to make a fresh start with Baker, and I agree."

"So, what about us? Are you still angry with me? I'm sorry," Claire says.

I smile, "No, I'm not. I'm not angry with Baker, either. I admit I was so mad at both of you, but now that I had time, I realize you were protecting me. Baker did not want me to know because, to him, it was something of the past, something that did not matter now."

"So, we're good then"? Claire says, smiling.

"Better than ever."

"I'm so happy you are back, Emma... Baker left you something on the office desk I think you should look at."

I start walking towards the office door, wondering what he could have left here for me. I open the door to the dark office. I flip the light on—a large envelope on the desk with both of our names. I sit in the desk chair and open the envelope to find pictures of Baker and me from the night of the Gala. I flip through them, and a single tear runs down my cheek, remembering the most fantastic night we had together. When I get to the end of the pictures, I realize one of them must be missing. I put them back into the envelope, and then I leave, taking them with me.

When I return to the front of the shop, Claire has finished cleaning up the shop and is getting ready to leave. I suspect she starts walking towards the office to grab her things to leave. “You want to get dinner? We could get some burgers. I know a great place,” I wink.

She laughs, “I don’t even have to answer that. You know I want to.”

After she grabbed her things, we locked up the shop and headed down the street to the bar that started it all.

Chapter Twenty-three

Baker

I'm angry that they did not tell me she was here of all places, but do I blame them? The whole reason I'm here is because of her. I finally got them to tell me the whole truth as to why she was there. My mother did not know everything that went down between Emma and me, and I appreciate that Emma did not come here to destroy me as a person. I knew she was better than that. It seems like my mother wanted to be there for her during a rough time, and I could not think of a better place for Emma to come to take her mind off everything that happened between us, Claire.

Speaking of Claire, after my conversation with my parents about Emma's time here, she messaged me to tell me that Emma was back in town, and they mended what was between them by going to the bar last night. I remember that night at the bar when I first met them and how this whole thing started. Knowing that Emma went there last night with Claire lets me know she is over what happened between us and is moving on from it.

I was walking out of my room from showering after a run along the beach when my father called me into his office to talk to me about something. "What is it that you want to talk about"?

I take a seat on one of his office chairs.

He reclines back in his desk chair. "I want you to know that I am proud of you, son. I'm proud of you for making the right choice by not taking the deal with Dave Riley. I know it was not an easy choice to make."

I look down at the ground before looking into his eyes. "Thanks, Dad. That means something to me, coming from you. You have always been there for us, helping us make the right decisions for the future of our company, and this was not easy. Ryan wanted this deal so badly, and I know he might be a little upset with me, but I needed to turn it down. It did not mean anything to me."

He gets a serious look on his face. "She loves you, son, and you doing this was just the thing that will bring her back to you."

"I hope your right, but how do you know that?"

He leans forward in his chair, putting his firsthand on the desk. "I just do. Now I know you had plans to stay here tonight, but I think you should head back home and contact Emma. She needs you."

I get up from my chair, "I don't understand."

He waves his hand, "There is nothing to understand, son. You need to make things right with her and get a fresh start on life with her."

"Thanks again. I guess I will get my things and head home. I will keep you and mom updated on how things go when I get back home" I start to walk out of his office.

"Baker," he says before I make it out.

I turn around, "Yea, Dad."

"Good Luck, son. I love you."

"Love you."

I walk out of his office, grab my things from my room, and after telling my mother goodbye, I head home to what I only hope can be Emma waiting for me.

Chapter Twenty-four

Emma

There are times when life sometimes needs something terrible to happen to make you realize all the right things in your life. These secrets that had been withheld from me only made me realize that my life is something so special to the people who love me, and I don't know that I can make it through the rest of my life without the people who have been loving and protecting me through all the terrible

I lost my parents, the most precious people in my life, and while I thought that meant that my life should stop, too, Claire was there to help me piece myself back together. These last few years with her by my side have been the best years of my life. She made me realize that I still have a life that I need to live. While it has been hard for me to want to live that life to the fullest, meeting Baker, loving me so easily, and showing me that there is so much more to my life that I never even thought I would want to live, a life of love.

My parents were so in love that I never once thought I would find someone to love me so much that I could have love just like them. I realized he loved me even though I was guarding my heart against him. Since giving him that second chance, he has not held his feelings back from me as I have for him. I'm

Emma Adler, loving someone I never thought I would fall for. I loved someone when I did not think that was possible. I wanted to go through the rest of my life just making it because I thought I couldn't be with someone without my parents here, but Baker has shown me that so many more people here on this earth can love me the way I need to be loved.

I have met not only him but also his remarkable parents, his mother, who has shown me that even though life gets tough, you take time to pick up the pieces and get back to where you need to be.

As I lay with my best friend Claire in my tiny apartment that I have called home the last few years, I realized that I could not hold back anymore. I want the life that Baker thoughtfully gave me. Today is the day I need him to know how much I love him.

"Claire, wake up," I'm standing on the side of the bed, my hands gripping her arms, shaking her.

She rolls over, her hair all over her face, "Emma, stop. What is it?" she sits up from the bed, pushing her hair back before putting on her eyeglasses from the side table.

"Claire, today is the day," I walk off into the bathroom connected to my room.

"Day for what?" she looks confused.

"I'm going to tell Baker I love him," I turn to her from the bathroom and see she is sporting a huge grin.

"Emma, I couldn't be happier for you."

She grabs the mug of coffee I had left for her on the side table and starts drinking it. "What is your plan?"

I'm standing in front of the mirror, brushing my hair out. I'm still in my pajamas and haven't even drunk the coffee I made for myself because I have been in panic mode all morning trying to come up with a better plan than I already had to tell him, but I can't think of anything.

"That's the thing, Claire. When I was at his parents, I thought, oh, I could tell him in the park because that's the place we were when he asked me to be his girlfriend. Still, then I thought, no, maybe that seems little, maybe I need to be more dramatic and big like he has been when he gifts me stuff, but then I can't think of anything because maybe I'm not that kind of person...."

"Slow Down, Emma, pause for a moment, breathe, and think of something. I mean, the park doesn't seem like a terrible idea. Doesn't he love you for being so simple? Maybe simple is just what you need to do then," Claire says.

I walk out of the bathroom and sit on the edge of the bed. I turn to Claire, "Maybe you're right. I should breathe and think of something" She laughs, "Emma, it'll come to you. Isn't he at his parent's for the weekend, though?"

"Catherine called me last night to tell me he came back yesterday, and he was coming back for me, but I haven't heard from him. What if he doesn't want me back? Maybe he realized he didn't love me. What if I took too long to realize that I love him?"

Claire sets down her mug on the table, then sits by me on the edge of the bed, "Listen, he loves you, Emma. I know he does because I've seen him since you have been apart, and you see it in his eyes that he was worried about you. He loves you more than anyone I have ever known. Maybe he is thinking of a way to get you back?"

Maybe he is thinking of a way to get me back, but this is my time to show him and prove that I love him.

"Claire, help me come up with a plan. Please" I give her a pouty lip, and she laughs.

"Let's do this!"

Chapter Twenty-five

Baker

I thought about Emma on the drive home after leaving my parent's house yesterday. When she wasn't here when I got here last night, It was tempting many times to get in touch with her. We can resolve our issues and get back together. I want to believe that my parents are right about her loving me but what if they're wrong? After going back and forth with my thoughts on the way home, I finally decided to let it be for the night and then decide what I wanted to do in the morning. Well, now that the morning is here, I'm just lying here thinking I should wait some more and see if she comes around.

I don't understand why this is becoming hard for me, I've been able to come up with all kinds of ideas for her, but now that it's come down to getting her back, I have a blank space in my thoughts. It's not that I don't want her because I want to be with her more than anything right now. It's just that I don't want to push something if she isn't ready, and if I need to wait a lifetime for her to come around, I will. I need to be more aware of Emma's feelings if we get back together. I know now how sensitive she can be because of some of the things she has gone through in her life. She can hold back during times I know she doesn't mean to.

I get out of bed and head into the bathroom to start the shower but find myself in her closet. I sit on the blush-colored ottoman in the middle of the closet. I lay back, looking up at the chandelier, and close my eyes. I picture in my head the day. The day I surprised her with this space, all for her, and I remember the look on her face. It's also where I found those awful bruises on her back. That was a hard time for both of us. She proved to me during that time that something so horrible was happening, of how strong she is. She's the strongest woman I know. She's been through battles I have never been through, and I know that she will get through whatever obstacles life throws her.

I get up from the ottoman, taking one last look around the closet before shutting off the light. I hope she will be here the next time I walk into this space.

Instead of the shower, I need to clear my mind by doing the one thing I know helps. I changed into running clothes, slipped on my tennis shoes, and headed down the elevator stairs.

Once I get started on the sidewalk, taking the route that takes me through the park, I realize I left my phone on my nightstand on my side of the bed. Instead of going back, I decide a day like today is the perfect time to run without distractions, so I don't go back for it.

When I make it to the park, I've been running for at least half an hour, so I walk through it instead of running so I don't run into anyone. I can't help but think I may see Emma here, and she once told me she loved walking through the park on her days off. I'm looking around to see if I can spot anyone who might look like her. I make it to the park's center, where benches surround a huge fountain. I see couples holding hands while walking through the park, reminding me exactly what I need to do.

I turn around, going back in the direction I just came from, and make my way out of the park. I ran home faster than I did earlier to get to the park. Once I get inside my building, I make my way up to my place. I run up the stairs and into my bathroom, where I shower to figure out the rest of my plan. I don't take my time in the shower and then dry off quickly before wrapping my towel around my waist.

Picking up my phone from my nightstand, I notice a missed message from Emma and open it immediately.

Emma: Meet me in the park. 8 pm tonight.

I didn't even get a chance to tell her myself, but that's precisely where I wanted to see her. I keep it short and tell her I'll be there. Now that I know I am finally going to get to see her, even though it's only been a week, I'm nervous and thinking about what I need to wear or do I need to bring her anything. There are only a few hours to decide everything and figure out exactly what I want to say to her.

Just before eight, Carlos pulls up from my apartment building to pick me up. I decided to wear something I would wear on a typical day for work: a polo and a pair of jeans.

I get into the car's back seat, shutting the door behind me. I am so nervous about what this meeting means for us. She could be standing there to tell me she enjoyed us, but I messed up, and she doesn't want to see me anymore. It could be the night she finally tells me the words I want to hear from her, or this could mean nothing. She could be standing me up for all I know, but she wouldn't do that.

I'm looking at my phone, scrolling the whole drive, but I'm getting nothing when I read the words I see on my phone, so I toss it to the side and look out the side window. After receiving her message earlier today, I cleaned up my whole place knowing there may be a slight chance she would come back home with me tonight. The thought of having her in my arms again while sleeping makes my heart skip a beat.

We pull up to the front entrance of the park, there isn't a car parked out front, and it makes me anxious, thinking she may not be here. Carlos opens my door for me to get out; once out of the car, I adjust myself and then clear my throat. Before I make my way to the entrance, he says, "She's waiting for you there."

Giving him a surprised look, I didn't know he even knew anything. I give him a nod and then take off for the park's entrance. I turn to watch him get back inside the car and drive off. When I reach the park, I notice there isn't a single person there, but when I look around, I spot her in the corner.

Standing in the gazebo, she is pacing back and forth without even noticing me. She is wearing a red flowy dress that comes just above her knees. Her hair is in a curly ponytail, and she has some sandals. I get closer to her, but she still hasn't noticed me yet, and she has a white piece of paper in her hand. I want to run to her, pick her up, swinging her around while kissing her, but I need to stay calm so she doesn't try to run off.

I finally get close enough that she turns to me when I say her name, giving me the biggest grin. She stops pacing and stands there, putting the white paper in her hand behind her back. I walk up the steps and finally come face to face with her. She holds her hand out for me to take, and without even thinking, I grab it only to realize my hand is sweaty. "Sorry" I take my hand from hers, wipe it on my pants, and then take her hand back into mine.

She is still sporting the biggest grin when she looks at me straight into my eyes. "Baker, thank you for meeting me here. I'm going to apologize in advance if whatever I say doesn't make sense or comes out the wrong way. I fully blame my nervousness,"

I let out a nervous laugh, and then she brought the paper behind her back so she could read it.

"Baker, I brought you here tonight to thank you for all you have done for me. I want to thank you for being who you are. I don't feel like I deserve someone like you,"

I stop her for a moment, which could go the way I don't want it to. "Em…" she holds up her hand to stop me, so I stop and continue to listen to her.

"When I first met you, I will be honest, and I didn't really like you. Before I knew you as who you were, I saw you as the type of guy who loves great things, only wanted to be with beautiful women, and had a reputation I wanted no part of. That night at the bar, I wanted to run as far away from you as possible and never see you again, but I was wrong. You proved to me these last couple of months that you are nothing like the person I thought you were. You have been everything to me. You helped save me when I didn't know I needed to be saved, you have shown me that you are a giving person, and I honestly will never be able to thank you enough for everything you have given me. Never in my life did I see myself falling in love with someone like you, but I did. I know it has taken me a long time to say that, but when I have gone through the things I have gone through in life, it's hard to love someone when you think you are just going to lose them. While I know I ran from you, I want you to know that I will never run from you again but will only look to you from now on. I can confidently say that my heart is yours to keep. I never want to go another day without you, and I want forever with you. I love you, Baker Hayes."

I wrap my arms around her, picking her feet up and spinning her around. "Forever… Em, I love you" then I kiss her lips, one that lets her know I have missed you.

I set her down on her feet, "I promise I will never let you down again. I'm so sorry for not telling you about the deal. This last week without you has been the hardest week of my life. I hope I never have to go another day without you in it. I love you so much, Emma Adler."

"I have to add one more thing," she says.

"What's that?"

She takes my hands in hers, "If the offer still stands… I want to sell my apartment and move in with you."

I wouldn't want this with her more. Placing both my hands on each side of her face, I bring her face to mine. "Not only does the offer still stand, but we can get our place, a place that we can pick together and call home," then I kiss her again.

While kissing her, I heard a familiar voice say, "Get a room," I turned to where the voice came from to find my parents, Audrey, Ryan, and Claire.

Surprised to see them all here, "What are all of you doing here?"

Emma grabs my hand, and we walk towards the gazebo stairs. "I invited them here. Well, they invited themselves here," she laughs. "When I talked to everyone today to ask for their help on how to tell you, they all insisted they needed to be here so that I couldn't tell them no. Ryan helped close the park down for the night. Claire helped me with my speech, and your parents played the biggest part in this. They took me in last week, and I couldn't be more thankful for them for helping me through a hard time. I love you guys," she blows a kiss to my mom.

Emma is the first to walk down the steps and instantly goes to my mother to hug her. I follow behind her.

My father reaches his arms out to me for a squeeze and then whispers in my ear, “I’m so happy for you, son. You got a good one, and I know there will be a lifetime of love between you.”

“Thanks, Dad”

I take Emma’s hand back in mine, “You want to get out of here… let's go home,” and she answers with a smile.

Chapter Twenty-Six

Emma

Two weeks. That's how long it's been since the night in the park, the night that I'll never forget. I never knew my heart could love someone as much as I love him. Since that night, we have been inseparable, looking for a new place to call home. It didn't take much convincing to get Baker to look for somewhere between our workplaces, and well, no more elevators. We needed a place we knew that Ryan couldn't make any more unannounced visits. It only took a few showings to find a spacious three-bedroom apartment with older charming details to make us say yes. Our new place also has Baker's only request: a kitchen with enough space for an occasional slow dance.

The day after leaving the park, Baker wasted no time getting my old apartment on the market, and it sold the next day. I guess it's a good thing to be dating New York City's best realtor. We moved all my stuff out after showings, and the next thing I knew, Baker already had us looking for our place. I couldn't be happier with our new place. It won't be a forever home for us, but it'll be the perfect place to grow.

Of course, Baker had to make a few changes to the new place, one being that I have a closet that replicated the one he had done for me at his old apartment. I insisted that that wasn't necessary, but he went through with the changes. I couldn't argue, I'll need the space for all the clothes I haven't even worn yet.

The movers finished up this afternoon, moving our furniture and boxes. We spent the rest of the afternoon just making a trail through the boxes and unpacking just some of our things so we could at least sleep here for our first night in our home together. I found the box with our sheets, so Baker ordered some Chinese takeout while I made the bed.

He walks into the bedroom just as I throw the duvet over the bed, the mattress on the floor for the night, so it doesn't take me long to make it. "Babe, the food shouldn't take long." He runs over to me, spinning me around to face him, and then pushes me, so we both fall on the mattress. Once we fall onto the bed, he moves the hair off my face with his hand, "Want to explore each other before the food gets here?"

I laugh, "Maybe after I shower. I'm not even sure I can get these clothes off with how sweaty I am now.

He scans the room, "I'm right there with you. We didn't get much done, but at least we can sleep here for the night and start unpacking first thing in the morning."

I use my hands to bring his face back to me so I can look him in the eyes. "I love you... I can't wait till we have this place feeling like home."

He kisses me while brushing his fingers across my forehead, "I love you more."

He gives me one more kiss before getting up off the bed, "I should go find us some glasses; we can pop the top of that bottle of champagne my parents got us to welcome us here. Let's celebrate our first night in our first place together."

"That's a great idea," I say, still lying on the bed but propped up on my elbows so I can watch him while he walks out of the room. Once he's gone, I shake my head with a smile before falling back onto the bed. While staring at the ceiling, my mind wondering off to the moment I met Baker and thinking just how I ended up here, and then I heard the top pop off the champagne bottle in the kitchen. I guess he found some glasses.

Getting up from the bed, I make my way to him, going down the hallway first and when I reach the kitchen, Baker stands holding up two glasses of champagne at the kitchen island.

"Looks like it didn't take you long to find those glasses," I say as I walk over to him to take one of the glasses from his hand.

"I got lucky. They just happen to be in the first box I opened."

"I would say you are a lucky man" I wink at him as I take a drink.

He takes the glass from my hand, setting it down on the counter with his own.

"Come here," he takes my hand into his, then wraps his arms around my waist. "Let's have our first dance in the new kitchen."

I take my hands, wrapping them up around his neck, laying my head against his chest while his arms wrap around my waist, slowly dancing.

"You are right, and I'm a fortunate man. I knew the first moment I saw you that I was going to love you for the rest of my life," he says

I laugh, knowing he couldn't see me smile if I did. "You knew the night at the bar that the girl wearing jeans, sneakers, and hair in a mess that was going to be your forever?"

"No," he pauses for a second, "I knew the moment I laid eyes on you at the coffee shop that you were the one for me."

I pause our dancing, leaning back to look at him. "The Brew House?... You saw me there, and you waited all this time to tell me."

"I remember the day very well. I was sitting at one of the back tables, waiting to meet a client. You came through the front door, your long blonde hair was down, and you wore a white shirt with jeans and sneakers. I couldn't take my eyes off you while you waited in line to order. I heard you ordered two iced vanilla lattes, and I couldn't help but think maybe one of those you ordered for a guy. While you waited for your drinks, my client called me about an emergency, and I took my eyes off you for one second. The bell at the front door went off, and that's when I saw you leaving. I ran to the door to see what direction you went off in and to run you down, but when I got out the door, you were nowhere. I thought that would be the last time I ever would see you, then when I went to the bar with Ryan that night, there you were. Fate, just like I told you the night of our first date."

I try holding the tears back that have built up, and our story isn't the one I had written in my head, a one-night stand after a night at the bar that also involved a deal. It is love at first sight, fate love story that you see in movies and read about in books.

"How come you never told me this? Does anyone else know?" We both start slow dancing again.

"I was waiting for the right time. I knew it was something I wanted you to know one day, and I just needed to wait for the right moment. No one else knew until yesterday," he lets go of me, going over to an open box on the floor from which he got the glasses. I turn around to watch him.

"There's something else I found in the box with the glasses. Give me a second to find it," Baker leans down to search around the box, and I wait, not knowing what it could be.

"Here it is." he pulls out a picture frame with the picture of us from the night of the Gala, the missing picture he kept, and it has sat on his nightstand every night since he got it.

"This is my favorite moment so far of us," he says, handing it over to me.

"Awe... Baker" I take it from him. "I love this picture so much... Hold on a second. I know just where to put this."

I walk down the hall, enter our room, and then run my fingers across it before setting it down on his nightstand. Once I come around the hallway corner, Baker is in the kitchen, sitting on one knee, holding open a small box, a ring. I immediately gasped, placing my hands over my mouth, tears falling down my face.

"Emma, I was saving that story for this moment, right here. I was serious when I said I knew that day that you were the one for me. Getting to know you beyond that day was just the icing for me. You mean more to me than anything, and I don't want to go another day of my life without you being mine forever. Emma Adler, will you marry me?"

I bend down to him, putting my hands around his neck, looking into his green eyes with my tear-filled eyes, "A thousand times, yes."

He gets up, wrapping his arms around me, picking me up off the ground. "I love you so much, Em."

"I love you, Baker Hayes... Something I never dreamed I would be saying, but here I am, and were engaged," I hold up my hand. He pulls the sizeable oval-cut diamond ring out of its box and places it on my finger.

"Engaged... I have been waiting for this day. I told everyone yesterday that today would be the day, which is why no one is here helping us move. I couldn't chance anyone spilling the news before I could ask you."

"Smart man, I know someone would've slipped, probably your mother," I laugh just as he puts me down to grab the two glasses filled with champagne on the counter. He hands me my glass, raising his, "Here's to our new home and being engaged" I raise my glass to his, toasting our new beginnings and then kissing him.

We spent the day today unpacking as many boxes as possible, and I put most of my clothes into my closet to have Baker help me find something to wear today. Bakers' parents insisted that we come over for dinner tonight, and I know they are probably throwing us an engagement party.

Once the car stops in front of his parent's house, I pause for a moment before getting out. The last time I was here, it was without Baker, and the sad memory of us apart comes to my mind. That memory seems so distant now that so much has changed with us since then. Baker comes to my door, opening it for me, "Come on, everyone is waiting for us."

I take his hand to get out of the car and walk through the front door. Not a single person is in sight when we get inside the house. We walk through the kitchen, and when we open the back door, everyone yells, "Surprise."

All his family and Claire are standing around the pool, and there's a large banner hanging above them that reads, Congratulations, Baker and Emma!

"Thank you, everyone," Baker says, taking my hand to greet everyone.

I reach Claire first, giving her a big embrace, and I feel like it's been forever since I have seen her.

Since Baker and I got back together, I had been so busy looking for a place and moving that I had only been in and out of the flower shop when I had free time. I think Baker hiring the two new girls was the best thing we have done with our business; this extra time off has been excellent.

"I'm so incredibly happy for you, Emma, maybe just a little bit jealous too," Claire says. "Don't be jealous. Your day is coming soon, I know it," she rolls her eyes, and I know it's because she hasn't had the best luck with boyfriends lately, but I know she will get her happy ending just like me.

Claire takes my hand, pulling me to the side while everyone else is still talking and greeting Baker with hugs. "He asked for my blessing before asking you to marry him. He asked me what I thought your dad would think of him. I want you to know that I told him that your dad would've loved him and that he would be so proud of you for finding someone to take the best care of you. I appreciate him asking me. I do. I know he is the best thing that has ever happened to you since losing your parents. I fully support you getting married, and I can't wait to have that same thing one day."

I couldn't have asked for a better person, a friend to go through life. I embrace Claire, "I love you, and I will never be able to thank you enough for being there for me through all these things in my life. I want you to know I will always be there for you too. Just because I moved doesn't mean we can't have more sleepovers. You call me, and I will be there."

"Thanks, Emma. Now we can finally plan a wedding. Let's not use any ideas we had when we were eight, though," we both laugh and join everyone else.

It's getting dark out, and it's a beautiful night for the party. After the most beautiful dinner that Catherine and Jack had prepared for us, we all sat around talking for a couple of hours. Baker decided to join his niece and nephew in the pool, so I found time to slip away from the party while no one noticed and take a stroll down to the beach.

Growing up by the ocean, there were many nights that I would take walks on the beach and sit under the stars. I would be down there for just a few minutes before my parents would come to join me. It was one of the many things I enjoyed doing with them. My dad would show up with a basket of snacks and drinks, and we would stay out there for hours just laughing and watching the stars. I remember seeing shooting stars, my dad always saying, "make a wish," and wishing for the things I have now. Those wishes included owning the flower shop with Claire, finding myself, and one day having a love like my parents. While I never really believed in wishing on a shooting star, I would always make a wish on them anyways. Now I know they really can come true. While I want my parents here so they can enjoy those things I wished on with me now, the memories of wishing those things while with them let me know they are watching over me.

I take my shoes off to walk easier in the sand, and once I reach the ocean, I take a seat and watch the stars just like I did on all those nights with my parents. It doesn't take long before I hear footsteps behind me; I guess I didn't slip away without someone noticing. I turn my head back to see Jack walking towards me. I turn back, remembering that one day on the beach and our conversation. His footsteps get closer, "Care if I join you?"

I pat the sand next to me, and he takes the seat. "Too many people at the party?"

"No. Just enough people. I just thought I would take advantage of this moment to come down to the beach."

"It's beautiful out here at night."

"It is... I used to go down to the beach with my parents at night all the time when I lived back home in Florida. I couldn't think of a perfect place to come to tonight" I don't take my eyes off the sky while talking to him.

"You know, I used to find Baker out here every night shortly after we moved in. He wasn't out of high school yet when we bought this place, and unlike most kids out making trouble every night, he would come out here to watch the stars, and sometimes I would join him, to check on him, and we would spend hours out here. He was a good kid and still is. I'm very proud of him, and you too, Emma. He's finally focusing on other things besides himself and work. There were many days that Catherine and I would think we would never see him fall in love, and here you are."

"Well, thank you, Jack" I keep it short but can't help but think about what he said about Baker. We both stay silent for a moment, looking at where the sky meets the ocean.

"Emma, we couldn't be more excited for you to join us and be your family," I look over at him this time while he talks.

"All of you already feel like family to me. I couldn't be more thankful for all of you, Ryan, too," I give Jack a small smile.

"Hey, there you are. I have been looking everywhere for you," I hear Baker's voice from behind us. Jack turns back to Baker walking towards us, and he gets up from the sand.

"I'll let you two have a moment," Jack says as he nods to Baker and then makes his way back to the house.

I start getting up from sitting in the sand, and Baker helps me up by grabbing my hand. "I just thought I would come out here for a minute since the party was down a little."

"It is great out here at night, isn't it...? Is everything okay?"

I smile, "Everything is good... perfect."

"Come, Ryan and I want to talk to you and Claire about something," Baker says as he walks back to the house with my hand in his.

As we make our way up to the house, I notice almost everyone is gone from the back patio besides Ryan and Claire. They are both seated in the dining chairs around the table. When we reach the table, Baker pulls a chair out next to Claire, and I take a seat. After he pushes my seat in, he walks to the other side of the table, sitting across from me, next to Ryan.

"Why do I feel like this is a business meeting?" I say, tapping my fingers on the table.

Baker gets a huge grin, "That's because it is."

I roll my eyes and then sit back in my seat. "What could you two possibly be up to now?"

Claire sits back, relaxed like she already knows what this little meeting entitles.

Baker leans forwards, resting his elbows on the table, holding his hands up. "Ryan and I here have looked over the numbers from what the Flower shop is earning and well spending…" he pauses.

"Go on, please. I would love to know what you have up your sleeve," I say, unimpressed. I've seen the numbers.

"Well, you two have quite the business, and the last couple of months' earnings tell us that you should open up a second location, or maybe just a bigger place, in a busier area."

"And…?"

Ryan leans over the table, "What Baker here is trying to say is that we just happened to see this nice building for sale last week, and we might have bought it for you two to have a second location."

I gasp, looking over at Claire and then back to Baker. "You what?"

Baker's smiling, "We want to invest in your business. Since we bought the building, which also happens to be next door to our business, we just figured we could help you expand your business to make more money. You've always said you needed a bigger place, so we bought you two a bigger place. So, you can discuss it together if you want to make this a second location or close the building you have now."

I look over to Claire, who is smiling. "You knew about this?"

"I mean, I just found out about it, but I think we should open the second location. You and I can take turns at the shop we have now and hire a couple more people to help us at the new one. They are right, though; we have been making a lot more money and have outgrown the shop we have now. What do you think?"

I think about it for a second, glaring at Baker. "Deal... Let's open the second location. But..." I put my hand up. "Claire and I get to make all the choices, you guys may own the place, but we have all the say. Got it?"

"Deal," they both say.

"You know what, I like this," I wave my hand around the table as we all get up from our chairs.

Baker says, "What is it about this that you like?"

The boys walk to the door to go into the house. Claire and I walk behind them, and I look over at her. She is smiling because she knows what I meant when I said it.

"Oh, nothing, never mind," I smile back at Claire.

If you think I would take back anything from my story about how I met and ended up with Baker Hayes, I wouldn't, not a second of it. This story started with a deal and ended with an even better one. Claire and I couldn't be happier, we got the dream we always wanted, and even though it's started somewhat rocky with these guys, they are taking the best care of us.

It only took a couple of days for Claire and me to pick out exactly what we wanted for the new flower shop, and the guys got to work on finalizing the building. We hired more new people and trained them at the small shop while the new one was under construction. Since Claire and I have always been together, we let Lexi and Liv run the old one together. At the same time, we work together in the new building but occasionally take turns to ensure the original store is still doing great. We couldn't close the shop that started it all for us. I want to think that maybe Lexi and Liv will get their story, just like Claire and me.

Before opening the new shop, Baker and I finally took that trip down to Sarasota that he bid on at the Gala. It was beautiful to show Baker my roots, where I grew up, and we ended the trip with a night on the beach, where I spent nights with my parents, watching the stars. Our trip was short, but Baker said he wanted to make sure it was a place we would always return to once a year.

While I love Baker so much and would marry him today if I could, we have decided to wait till next summer to have our wedding, and if you guessed that it's going to be happening on the beach in the Hamptons, you guessed right. Catherine would want nothing more than for us to say our I dos in her backyard. I can't argue with her. I can't think of a better place to have it. Claire will be by my side that day as my maid of honor, and I can't wait. She has already been worrying about who will be her date, and while I told her she doesn't need one, she insisted on my help finding her one. So, here I stand at the front counter of the new flower shop with Claire and doing what you would think, making her a profile on a dating app.

"What do you think sounds better? Watches episodes of *Golden Girls* while eating ice cream from the tub or having sleepovers with my best friend on the weekends?"

I laugh while taking her phone from her hand, "Seriously, Claire, neither one. How old are you again?... How about we say you own a flower shop and love spending the weekend relaxing in the Hamptons? I mean, that isn't a lie. I don't think the other two things will get you a date."

She takes the phone back and starts typing what I just told

her. I leave the counter to grab my purse from the office so I can walk next door to eat lunch with Baker.

"Emma, I can feel it. I will meet the love of my life on a dating app," She yells out as I grab my stuff.

I laugh as I walk back to the counter, "Good Luck with that. You will meet the love of your life soon, dating app or not. I just know it."

She's swiping on profiles already, "Thanks, Emma, Have a good lunch. I'll see you when you get back."

She leans over the counter, still swiping profiles and not paying attention to anyone else. I push the door open and say to myself, "But what if you've already met him."

Bonus Chapter

Baker

Walking toward The Brew House, a coffee shop in New York City, I grumble under my breath, "Fucking Ryan."

I needed him more than anything this morning to take this client because I had a long list of things to do. Instead, Ryan stayed out all night with his latest chick, and apparently, things got heated between them. So, here I am, being the responsible brother and taking on a meeting with Ryan's client at the coffee shop. He needs to get his shit together soon.

Once inside, I walk straight to the back of the shop and sit at a small table. Pulling my laptop out of my bag, I set it down in front of me to open it. Then turn it on.

This place isn't my typical meeting place, but Ryan was the one who set this meeting up.

I hear the jingle of the bell above the front door as it opens and in walks a woman: with long blonde hair, simple clothing, and tennis shoes. My eyes look up at her and don't leave. She's leaving me.... It's unexplainable. I listen as she walks over to the counter, ordering two vanilla iced coffees. Large. Are those for her and a man? I look at her hand, not seeing a ring on either. She's not taken but should be by me. Did I think that, considering that is something that's never crossed my mind before?

She walks over to the side to wait for her coffee, and I still can't take my eyes off her. She looks around, probably because she can feel me looking at her, so I look down at my laptop for just one second. Then I start hearing a vibrating sound on the table, but instead of looking at it, my eyes flick right back up to her. What's her name, and where is she going?

The sound coming off the table from my phone doesn't stop, and I look down to answer finally.

"Hello, Baker Hayes," I say, holding the phone to my ear.

"Listen, Baker, I'm sorry to do this, but I won't be able to make the meeting this morning. We had something come up," the client says.

Shit, did everyone have something come up this morning? It looks like I do too.

I look down at my laptop for a second, forgetting I'm on the phone and trying to remember who I was meeting this morning.

"Do what?" I say.

That's when I noticed she was gone. The woman is no longer standing, waiting for coffee. She left.

I rush over toward the door and push it open. Looking in both directions, I search for her and anything that resembles her.

"Hello, Baker? Are you there? Did you hear me?" the client on the phone says.

I shake my head, "Sorry. Uh, that's okay. I'll have Ryan get in touch with you," I say before hanging up.

"Shit," I say before pushing the coffee shop door back open.

Whoever that woman was has left me feeling shaken. I needed to talk to her, ask her name, and introduce myself, but I didn't get the chance. This feeling is not a feeling I've felt from just one look. Could she have been a *forever*? I'll never know because I may never see her again.

I gather my stuff off the coffee shop table and leave.

What a morning. Thanks, Ryan.

When I went to the office, the woman from the coffee shop never left my mind. I've thought about her all day, and it's starting to wear on me. Baker Hayes doesn't do love, but why do I feel like there could've been something there between me and someone I've never met in my entire life? Hell, I don't know a single thing about her except for her looks.

Obviously, Ryan had a bad day because now I'm at The Bar. Another place I don't usually come to unless Ryan feels like shit from his life choices. Hence, the four shots he's already taken. I should be joining him, but I don't feel like being bad tonight.

"Ryan, have you ever seen a woman and thought she was the one?" I ask.

Ryan and I have been sitting at the bar top for an hour now. Neither has talked about anything other than work. I don't intend to ask about what's going on in his personal life because we usually don't talk about that stuff.

He laughs, "Who are you, and what have you done with my brother?"

"Forget it," I take a sip of the beer I've been nursing for the past thirty minutes.

"So, I've been thinking," Ryan says.

"Don't start. Don't even think about telling me you have this amazing plan because your life is shitty right now, Ryan. I don't have time for this."

"Hear me out. You want to impress Dave Riley, right?"

I don't think Ryan has ever had a great idea, but I always listen. So I say, "Go on."

"What if you and I got women, not girls? Like actual women with great jobs. They also obviously have to be pretty. But anyways, what if we show Dave that we are better than what he thinks of us? We show him that we aren't sleeping around...."

I interrupt, "You mean you sleep around."

He rolls his eyes, "Anyways, before you rudely interrupted me. We show Dave that we can be good guys by getting great women to stand by our sides. The buildings will be ours before the end of the year, and we can be wealthy,"

"We're already wealthy."

"Don't you want to be like a stupid rich asshole? Listen, you know you want to, so why don't we go ahead and look around this bar."

"You've gotta be kidding me. This bar is a hell hole, Ryan. You won't find a pretty girl here."

"Here or Deuce? You choose. We can leave here right now." he says, pointing thumbs at me.

I pretend to scan the bar, but I'm trying to think of a better plan than what Ryan has put before me. We've been working together on how to buy these buildings from Dave Riley for months. I'm starting to get impatient with this whole process. Finding a woman to be by my side isn't a bad idea as long as she makes the process worth it.

I turn my attention back to Ryan, "Nothing."

I wasn't looking. A pretty girl could be here, but my mind wants the woman I saw this morning.

Ryan turns around on his barstool, "Fine. I'll find some. First, I've gotta take a leak."

"You're dumb, you know that," I say.

Ryan gets up from the barstool and toward the bathrooms at the back of the bar. I need a minute to myself, so I sip my beer while I wonder what has gotten into me today.

The Bar is a total gentlemen's bar, and I highly doubt Ryan will find someone. The idea he has come up with doesn't sound too bad. I've always had this reputation with people thinking I'm always with different women. I may be on the newspaper's front cover with someone different all the time, but those are just meeting with clients that have been taken out of context. I've held the role of letting people think that's who I am because I don't choose to tell them any different.

Yes, I've been with different women, not as many as Ryan, but enough. And none of them have been serious relationships, purely just sleepovers. Today has shown me that maybe I'm ready for something serious.

Ryan sits back at the bar and throws a wave at the bartender, "Can we get two shots to the women at the back of the bar?"

"Holy shit, Ryan. No." I yell out.

"Trust me. They are good ones. I've never been into

redheads, but the one at the back of the bar caught my attention. Have a look for yourself?"

"I'm leaving. This deal isn't going to work with me."

"Baker, look. I promise you. They are the women for the job."

Hesitant, I turn around, and there she is. The woman at the back of the bar is from this morning. I don't want to admit it, but my brother is the best. Thank you for the stupid plan, Ryan. Maybe it isn't so dumb after all.

"You've got the blonde, right?" Ryan asks me.

"Yea. I've got her," I smirk.

This night just got a thousand times better.

She's here.

You know, in your life, you have those highs in lows all on the same day, and you don't know what direction your day ends up. Yeah, my day is going to finish on a high. I already know it.

I've been sitting here with the most amazing woman, in this booth, across from my stupid but sometimes comes up with good plans, brother. We've all been here for hours.

Her name is Emma, and I've already given her my name for her. "Em."

Ryan has been flirting with her friend Claire, and I'm just trying to get any information from Emma that I can get, but it looks like she doesn't like to talk much about herself. I want to know more. I need to.

I've already seen the effect I've had on her tonight, and I know I will not want this night with her to end here at the bar. I don't want to sleep with her, but I do want to see where tonight goes.

It does seem that Emma knows about me, but she doesn't know the real me. She knows the me that everyone else thinks I am. I have my work cut out for me when it comes to letting her know who I really am and can be for her.

After a few shots and beers, it's time to call it a night.

"Want us to give you a ride home?" I ask.

"That's okay. We aren't far from here. We can walk," Emma says.

She's not thinking right now. No way on earth I'd let her walk home from this bar. She's going with me.

"Sorry, but I can't let you two do that after drinking... Claire, Ryan can drop you off and Emma. You're coming with me," I say

The look on Emma's face tells me she doesn't like what I just said, but I want more time with her. If I let her leave, there's a chance I'd never see her again, and I don't want to risk that. I don't want to feel like I did this morning when she left the coffee shop.

Once we all say goodbyes and Ryan and Claire take off, I text Carlos to let him know where coming out the front.

After putting my phone back in my pocket, I take Emma's hand and lace our fingers together. Our hands mold together perfectly. This feeling seems so natural as we walk out of The Bar together.

Once we walk inside my penthouse, I know already I'm

giving off the impression that I am precisely who people say I am with this place. Having a driver get us also wasn't ideal either. She knows I have money, and sometimes that's something I don't like about myself. My money is what's going to run her off.

"Want anything?" I ask.

She shakes her head no while spinning around to look over my place.

I take a seat on the leather sofa, and she joins me.

"Your place is probably the nicest place I've ever been," she says, nervous.

"Thank you. I know this doesn't make me look good to you right now, but I promise I'm not the typical has money, and also, I'm an asshole kind of guy."

She smiles, making me feel tingly in the chest, throwing me off with my feelings. Is this what happens when you like someone?

"Anything you want to do?" I ask, reaching over to take her hand, thinking it may make her more comfortable with me.

She turns her body in my direction on the sofa, "Can I ask you something?"

I sit straight up and look into her eyes, our hands still together, "Ask me anything?"

"It's probably the drinks or me being here in your home, but I want to know what it's like to kiss Baker Hayes," She looks deeper into my eyes.

God, I want this, I do, but I'm not someone special. I'm just me. All the other women think this when they are with me too, but she's different. If anything, I want to know what it's like to kiss her.

"Yes," I say because I can't say no now. "I want to kiss you," I add, so I don't look like an idiot.

I lift my back off the couch and lean into her. Taking her face into my hands, she wets her lips before biting down on her bottom lip. She is nervous. I'd be a dumbass to think I'm not nervous about doing this with her. Is this where I thought I would end up when I saw her this morning?

I take one deep breath and then put my lips to hers while holding her face in my hands. Her lips are soft, and it doesn't take a second for her to open her mouth, giving me more access. Giving her more of me makes me weak in the knees. She is everything. This is everything

I pull back to give myself a second to breathe. I could go like this all night with her.

"Disappointing?" I ask.

She smiles before shaking her head no.

Gosh, she's beautiful and the woman you bring home to your mom. She's everything I want, and I still know nothing about her. If she leaves now, I will need to see her again and again. Date her, except I don't date. But her, I'd do it for her.

She leans back into me, and her lips come back to mine. This time she kisses me more, I take control by taking her face in my hands again. I stop us once more.

"Emma, I like you," I brush her hair back from her face.

She looks down at her hands in her lap, "Thank you."

Lifting her chin with my hand, "Stay with me tonight?"

Her eyes meet mine again, "You sure?"

"I don't think I've ever been so sure of anything."

She nods, and I lean forward, placing a kiss on her lips.

I don't know what tonight holds for us, but I hope it's the start of something great, not only for me but for us. I meant it when I told Emma I liked her. Tonight is just the beginning of getting to know her.

Printed in Great Britain
by Amazon